TUESDAY, SEPTEMBER 8

On the morning of her fortieth birthday, Bernadette McBride woke up twelve again. It didn't dawn on her immediately. As the sun slanted across her narrow bed, what Bernadette first felt was the stiff cotton sheets drawn up under her chin. Sheets that had been starched and smelled of lavender.

Odd, she thought. Who starches sheets anymore?

"Bernadette!"

That sounds like my mother, she thought. *Oh, how I wish it were.* In her hazy state of half-waking, she tried to remember the last time she had heard her mother's lilting voice: Was it the day before she died? She had called on the telephone to ask Bernadette if she would drive her to the garden store.

"Are you up?" Another shout from downstairs.

That *is* my mother's voice, Bernadette thought. How could that be?

OTHER BOOKS YOU MAY ENJOY

12 Again

Sue Corbett

PUFFIN BOOKS

PUFFIN BOOKS
Published by the Penguin Group
Penguin Young Readers Group, 345 Hudson Street, New York, New York 10014, U.S.A.
Penguin Group (Canada), 90 Eglinton Avenue East, Suite 700, Toronto, Ontario, Canada M4P 2Y3
(a division of Pearson Penguin Canada Inc.)
Penguin Books Ltd, 80 Strand, London WC2R 0RL, England
Penguin Ireland, 25 St Stephen's Green, Dublin 2, Ireland (a division of Penguin Books Ltd)
Penguin Group (Australia), 250 Camberwell Road, Camberwell, Victoria 3124, Australia
(a division of Pearson Australia Group Pty Ltd)
Penguin Books India Pvt Ltd, 11 Community Centre, Panchsheel Park, New Delhi - 110 017, India
Penguin Group (NZ), Cnr Airborne and Rosedale Roads, Albany, Auckland 1310, New Zealand
(a division of Pearson New Zealand Ltd)
Penguin Books (South Africa) (Pty) Ltd, 24 Sturdee Avenue,
Rosebank, Johannesburg 2196, South Africa

Registered Offices: Penguin Books Ltd, 80 Strand, London WC2R 0RL, England

First published in the United States of America by Dutton Children's Books,
a division of Penguin Young Readers Group, 2002
Published by Puffin Books, a division of Penguin Young Readers Group, 2007

1 3 5 7 9 10 8 6 4 2

CIP Data is available.
ISBN: 0-525-46899-4 (hc)

Puffin Books ISBN 978-0-14-240729-5

Printed in the United States of America

For my sweetie pie, Tom;
the cookie monsters, Conor and Liam;
and for Brigit, aka Princess Cupcake

The author gratefully acknowledges the assistance provided through the Knight Fellowship for Journalists at Stanford University (especially the generosity, foresight, and wisdom of the two Jims in allowing spouses to participate), where this novel began in the inimitable Keith Scribner's fiction-writing class. Thanks, too, to Eavan Boland, Jason Brown, David M. Kennedy, Rob Polhemus (rhymes with "genius"), and Tobias Wolff, for generously opening their classes to me.

A big thank-you to all who offered vital words of encouragement: John Dufresne, who read the first two chapters and said, "I'd read more."

The TabbWriters: Joanne Dingus, Cathlin Parker, Karen Dudden-Blake, Joan Sprigle-Adair, and, especially, Michelle Leonard, who said, "Maybe your second chapter is your first."

My darling sister, Mary Jean, who said, "*When* this is published . . . "

Tom, who said it was okay for me to quit my day job. Well, one of them.

To Beth, Jacquie, Shari, and Lisa, who said, "You go, girl," and sent the bubbly when I got there.

And to Meredith, who said, "Yes."

How stunning are the changes which age makes in a man while he sleeps.

—MARK TWAIN

12Again

Patrick's Story

LABOR DAY, SEPTEMBER 7

Patrick's mother vanished on Labor Day, the day before her birthday, the day before he started seventh grade.

"*Technically,* yes, it's a holiday," she had said at breakfast. "But, *realistically,* newspapers have no holidays. See? The newspaper arrived today like it does every day. And I have a story due Wednesday that is nowhere near ready to give to an editor tomorrow, so I'm working."

"I'm in charge," Patrick's father had said, looking over the top of the business pages at Patrick and his brothers. "Whatever you boys need, come to me."

Patrick didn't need anything. He had plans. He and his two best friends would ride bikes to Jones Beach, swim until they were waterlogged, then play football on the sand. A *perfect* last day of summer vacation. He couldn't wait.

But just as the breakfast dishes were being cleared from the table, Gerard McBride's beeper vibrated on the counter, rattling the air.

"It's the hospital," he said, looking at the illuminated read-out. Patrick's father was the obstetrician on call. He picked up the telephone, pushed the buttons automatically, and identified himself. Patrick quickly folded the sports section and dropped it on the table. He raced upstairs to get dressed. If he could get out the door before his father got off the phone . . .

"Patrick!" He heard his mother calling.

"I'm not dressed," he shouted down the stairs.

"Come back here, please."

Darn it! Patrick thought. He knew what was coming. He trudged down the stairs, shorts on, T-shirt in his hand. If only he had skipped reading the newspaper. He could've been gone by now.

"I'm sorry, Bernadette," Patrick's father had said, replacing the phone in its cradle. "Mrs. Lee's blood pressure has shot through the roof. I'm going to have to deliver that baby right now." Gerard washed his hands in the kitchen sink and left.

"You don't have any plans, do you?" his mother asked, turning to Patrick.

"Yeah, I do—" He stopped. Patrick wasn't allowed to ride his bike to Jones Beach, so he couldn't say that. "I'm doing something with Kyle and Duffy."

"Doing what?"

"I don't know. Something."

"Well, it'll have to be something that includes Neil," his mother said, slotting dirty plates into the dishwasher. "Maybe you can take him to the high school and play base-ball."

"*Mom,* it's the last day of vacation," Patrick complained. The *last* thing he wanted was to hang out with his little brother all day.

"I know, Patrick, but it can't be helped. It's just until your father gets back. Maybe it will be a quick delivery."

"Quick? When has it taken less than a couple of hours? It'll take the whole morning, and then it'll be too late to do anything," Patrick said, slumping into a kitchen chair. As soon as I get old enough not to *need* a baby-sitter, Patrick thought, now I have to *be* the babysitter.

"Patrick, give me the morning," his mother said in a pleading tone, crossing to the table. "If I can get most of my assignment done, then you can have the afternoon with your friends." She tried to ruffle his hair, but Patrick ducked under her arm, got up, and left the room. He was too old to have his hair ruffled.

Typical, thought Patrick. Neil agreed to play baseball, all right—for about fifteen minutes.

"I'm thirsty," he told Patrick, who was pitching to Kyle. "Did you bring anything to drink?"

"No."

"Mom always brings things to drink," Neil said.

"Well, I'm not Mom. Go back to the infield," Patrick told him.

"This is boring," Neil answered, scuffing the grass with his feet on the way back to second base.

"I agree," Kyle shouted. He gestured for Patrick to walk toward home plate. "Can't you ditch him at home? We still have time. . . ." he whispered.

"What time is it?"

Duffy had trotted in from the outfield. "Nine-thirty," he said.

"No, I can't take him home yet. You guys should just go to the beach without me. Where're you going to be?"

"How about Field Four?" Duffy suggested.

"Okay. Meet me at the concession stand at Field Four at one o'clock," Patrick said.

"You sure?" Duffy asked.

"Yeah. See ya then," Patrick said, stuffing his bat, his ball, and his mitt in his sports bag as Duffy and Kyle pedaled off toward the woods. Patrick watched them disappear in a plume of dust spun up by their tires. There was a bike path just beyond the line of trees at the edge of the high-school property. They'd take it all the way to Wantagh Parkway and the beach.

"C'mon, squirt," he said, turning to Neil.

"Mom said not to call me that."

"Mom's not here."

Patrick spent the morning serving Neil, who spilled the juice Patrick got him and needed a sponge, a napkin, and then a clean shirt. He wanted the crayon box down from the top shelf of his closet, the lid pried off, paper to draw on, Scotch tape to hang up his picture on the refrigerator, a glass of milk, a snack, help with his zipper, help getting a different box down, somebody to play Clue with him. A nonstop needfest, thought Patrick.

At noon, he poked his head into his mother's office.

"Neil wants to know when lunch is," he said.

"Oh, Patrick—lunch." She looked frazzled. "Do you know how to get this stupid thing to unfreeze? I forgot to save the work I already did, and now the cursor won't budge."

"Did you try **Control-Break**?"

"About thirty times."

"Then you gotta reboot."

"Arrrrgggh," she said, letting her forehead hit the keyboard. "I *hate* computers." She flicked the power switch, and the screen pulsed and went dark. "Two hours of work, totally wasted."

"So what should I tell Neil about lunch?"

"I'm coming. Your father called."

"He's on his way home?"

"No. He said his patients were taking Labor Day literally. He's delivered two already, another woman is in labor, and one more is on her way in."

"So am I off duty now?"

"Hello? Did you not hear what I just said?"

"But you said earlier, 'Just give me the morning.' "

"But that was because I made the ridiculous assumption this computer would not eat everything I already wrote! I'm sorry, Patrick. I'm not happy about it either."

Patrick finished his lunch and put his dish and glass in the dishwasher. His mother had already retreated to her office. Kevin, his other brother, watched his fourth hour of TV.

The doorbell rang, and through the living-room window he could see a Pest-Away van in the driveway.

"Mom! The bug guy's here," Patrick called up the stairs.

"But it's Labor Day!"

"Well, he's here. Should I tell him *technically* it's a holiday?"

"I'm coming." She went to the door, and Patrick saw her shoulders slump as she talked to the guy, who had a gas mask noosed around his neck. She was nodding. "Just give us a couple of minutes, okay?" she said, shutting the screen door. Then she turned and walked to the couch, where Patrick sat with Kevin and Neil, watching TV.

"He's backed up because of the rain last week."

"So what does that mean?" Patrick asked.

"It means we gotta clear out of here so he can spray. Bran, too."

"But, Mom," Kevin said. "This show just started."

"For goodness' sake, Kevin, it's *Hawaii Five-0.*"

"Well, there's nothing else on but soap operas," he answered.

"Kevin, look outside—it's a brilliant day. Why don't you *do* something instead of polluting your brain with that nonsense?"

"There's nothing to do!" Kevin said.

"There's *plenty* to do," his mother answered. "Why, I could come up with a hundred things to do if *I* had nothing to do."

"Mom, that doesn't make any sense," Patrick said.

"Please get the dog, Patrick."

By late afternoon, Patrick saw his mother had that don't-push-me look. She was in the kitchen, washing out the nylon lunch bags they hadn't used since school ended in June. Neil had parked himself in front of the TV with Kevin, so

Patrick retreated to the garage to play his electric guitar. The door from the kitchen opened and she yelled, "Patrick!" giving him the thumbs-down sign. Too loud.

"If it's so loud, how come I can still hear you yelling at me about how loud it is?" Patrick muttered, but she had already turned her back. He twisted the dial left. A little. He had learned not to cross his mother. She'd pull the plug.

But Patrick had to play loud enough to drown out the stuff *she* listened to—every song a whine about a broken heart or a busted dream. She sang along with the radio and Patrick couldn't decide which was worse: the fact that she was off-key or that you could hear her Long Island accent when she was singing about honky-tonks. Once, he'd caught her singing into a wooden spoon. It was so . . . embarrassing.

"As soon as you three are off to college, I'm getting a fringed skirt, a guitar, and heading to Nashville," he'd heard her say, more than once. "Your father will be my business manager."

Patrick ignored remarks like this, but Kevin encouraged her, channel-surfing until he found some guy in a hat singing about how he couldn't kiss his girlfriend because his mouth was full of chew. Powerfully bad music seemed to be the only thing on TV that interested his mother, whereas Kevin was drawn to TV like flies to rotting food.

Patrick was slicing cucumbers when his father finally walked through the door. His mother had just taken a pizza out of the oven. Kevin had been ordered to stop watching TV. Instead, he was sitting at the kitchen table, fighting aliens on his Game Boy.

"Two boys and two girls today," his father said as they sat down at the table. His mother was quiet. "Did you get your story done?" he asked.

"Ha!" she snapped.

"I'll take that as a no," his father said. "Well, how was everybody else's last day of summer vacation?" he asked.

"Lousy," Patrick said.

"Boring," Neil said.

"Kevin?" his father asked.

"The Mets game wasn't on TV," he said.

"Okay, I guess it's a good thing summer's over, then," his father said. No one laughed. "Patrick, pass the salad, please. I'm sure you're all excited about starting school tomorrow."

"Is there something to be excited about?" Kevin asked.

"I hope the teacher isn't mean," Neil said. "Bobby Yablonski had Mrs. Green last year and he called her Mean Green."

Patrick's father poured salad dressing over his lettuce. "Neil, you need to give Mrs. Green a chance. I'm sorry I won't be able to meet her myself tomorrow," he said.

His mother dropped her fork to her plate. "But aren't you off? You were on call all weekend." Patrick stopped eating, too.

"I have an early flight to Albany for that obstetrics conference," Gerard told her, between bites. "I told you that already, right?"

"Is that a joke?" she asked.

"I didn't tell you?" Dad asked.

Patrick cleared his throat to try to get his father's attention.

"No, you didn't," his mother said. Patrick kicked his father's foot, but his father kept his attention focused on his mother.

"It's a one-day thing. I should be home by dinner."

Finally, Patrick leaned toward his father. "Dad," he whispered. "Tomorrow is Mom's birthday."

"Your birthday! Oh, Bernadette, I am an idiot. I *completely* forgot," he said. "We'll do something this weekend, okay?"

Bad move, Dad, Patrick thought. If only he had just *offered* to skip the conference. His mother would have said not to bother. But from the look on her face, Patrick knew the fact that Dad had forgotten her birthday had pushed his mother past some breaking point. She returned Patrick's glance but did not say anything. She stood, picking up her plate. He watched her as she crossed the kitchen, lifted the trash-can lid, and tilted her plate so her half-eaten pizza slid into the garbage. He looked sideways at his father, who met his eyes.

"Bad day around here?" his father asked.

"Right," Patrick answered.

"I'm going to my mother's house," his mother announced.

"Why is Mom going to Grandma's?" Neil asked. His father opened his mouth to talk, but his mother answered the question.

"Because it's quiet!" she said, leaving the room. "And because there are no unpleasant surprises there!"

"Ooooh, Pops, you're in trouble," Kevin said. "You know, you can send flowers for any occasion by calling 1-800-SEND-FTD."

"The florists of America thank you for paying such careful attention to their advertising campaigns, Kevin," his father said.

"Happy to help."

Patrick thought about his grandmother's empty house. He had only been there a few times since her funeral six months ago. They used to go there several times a week, mostly to drop off groceries. His grandmother was the weirdest person Patrick had ever known—"The Hermit," neighborhood boys called her, because she almost never left the house. But she was great fun. She doted on Patrick and told him stories. She believed in magic and fairies, and until Patrick got older, she had him believing those things existed, too. Sometimes, he still wondered about all the odd things that happened when she was around. Once, for instance, when Patrick was about six, he had mentioned that he and Kevin wanted a dog, but Mom had said not until Neil was out of diapers.

"A boy ought to have a dog," his grandmother had said in a huff. Then she walked to a corner of her garden and grabbed a handful of straw. From what Patrick had seen, it looked like she was smashing the hay into a ball, but when she turned around there had been no hay—only a chocolate-brown puppy with bits of hay in his fur.

"This is Bran. He's yours, but you can keep him here until your ma is ready."

"Where did you get him, Grandma?" Patrick had asked her as the pup splayed his small paws across Patrick's chest, tucking his soft head right under Patrick's chin.

"He'll need a dish of milk," was all she'd said. "Run in the house now and I'll get a box for him to sleep in." Patrick

never asked about Bran's origins again, but he had heard
mother ask the same question. She didn't get an answer either.

Patrick did the dishes and then went to his room. What a
wasted day. He put his headphones on and stretched out on
his bed. He heard a knock and the door opened. His mother
stood at the threshold, an overnight bag and her laptop in its
carrying case looped over her shoulder. She looked like she
was about to say something, and Patrick waited for her
to give him some chore or lecture—but she never did. She
didn't say anything. Not a word.

And then she was gone.

BERNADETTE'S
STORY

EVENING, LABOR DAY

Bernadette McBride looked in her rearview mirror as she backed out of the driveway and saw only the dark, empty night. What a rotten day. Not only had she not gotten a thing done, she had spoiled Patrick's day, too. She would have to rethink this arrangement of working at home.

When the boys were younger she had wanted to be home to take them to piano lessons or help with homework, and she had been. She *and* her cell phone *and* her beeper *and* her laptop—checking e-mail while Kevin learned to bunt; proofreading a story while Patrick had a karate lesson.

But it was becoming harder to get anything done. Today had been typical—all the disruptions. Bran wanting out, then in. Neil, needing an audience for everything, bringing her one arts-and-crafts project after another—each suggesting another creative mess waiting somewhere for her to clean up.

"I made these for you," he had told her that afternoon, presenting her with a bouquet of flowers crafted from coffee filters and pipe cleaners.

"Why, thank you, Neil. Are there any coffee filters left now?"

"No. But we could recycle these!" he had said, thrilled at discovering another project.

"Great idea, but let's only recycle the ones you didn't put Magic Marker on, okay?" she asked. He had already run off.

Bernadette cut through the shopping center, then took a left on West Drive into her mother's neighborhood. She still couldn't believe Gerard had totally forgotten she was turning forty. She wished *she* could forget it.

"You're angry," he had said, when he followed her out to the car.

"No, it's just that I'm going to have to pull an all-nighter to finish this story," she answered, opening the car door and tossing in her bag and her laptop. Actually, she was too tired to stay angry and too tired to forgive him completely. "But, Gerard, would I forget *your* birthday?"

"No, you wouldn't, but I will make it up to you—Saturday night. I'll plan the whole thing," he said, circling her waist with his arms. "You'll feel, um—thirty-eight!—all over again."

She laughed and looked up for a kiss. "If you have the power to change my age, please make me *much* younger," she said. "Then I can be your trophy wife and we can take a vacation with the money you don't have to pay the divorce lawyers."

Bernadette parked her station wagon in the driveway and, by the light of the full moon, found the key on her ring. Her mother's house was at the end of a cul-de-sac and backed up to a stretch of empty woods. Under the curtain of evening, she could barely see it, dwarfed by darkness, tall trees, and the homes around it.

Fiona Downey's house was the only one on William Street that resembled its humble, original self. The neighbors had added dormers and dug swimming pools. Her mother had resisted change. There was no microwave or dishwasher. For Christmas one year, long after everyone but Bernadette had left home, her brothers and sister gave their mother a dryer, a gift Fiona failed to appreciate.

"The wash will smell of metals," she had said. "What did God make breezes for?"

Since her mother's death in March, Bernadette had avoided the house she grew up in, though over the years she had walked there countless times, often pushing a baby stroller to get a cranky child to nap.

She knew it would fall to her to put her mother's life into boxes and give it away, but she lacked the will to begin. Bernadette, the only one among her siblings who hadn't left the neighborhood, the state, the time zone, was not good at getting rid of things. It was hard just to be *in* the house without her mother there. She couldn't bring herself to empty it of her mother's things.

She opened the gate to the backyard because she always went into the house through the kitchen door. Her mother had held on to some sort of superstition about the front door. Her mother had had a lot of superstitions. She had warned Bernadette against picking up pennies unless they were heads up. A wallet given as a gift had to have money in it, otherwise it foretold poverty. Fiona had believed in ghosts but not doctors, and had treated coughs and stomachaches with concoctions she cooked up on the stove.

Neighbors had always considered her eccentric, but Bernadette never believed it was as benign as that. Bernadette was ten when her father left, and her mother had cursed him. Literally, Bernadette believed. He did not prosper, and his children rarely heard from him again.

Bernadette flipped on a light in the kitchen and dropped her bag into a chair. Her mother's kitchen was thoroughly altered by her absence—the radio silent, the stove cold, the kettle empty. It gave Bernadette the chills, because she could close her eyes and picture her mother here—kneading bread on the counter, or sitting at the small table, peeling an orange.

Though it was early September and still warm, Bernadette lit a fire, out of habit. After putting water on to boil for tea, tending the fire was always the next thing her mother had done when she came in.

Bernadette made sure the flue was open and struck a match to the kindling. Smoke rose in the grate, then the fire took, leaves curling in on themselves and licking the sides of a log she had placed on top of some twigs. The neighbors will think my mother's ghost is here, she thought, and the idea warmed her. If my mother *were* still alive, Bernadette thought, she would have gladly kidnapped Neil for the day, and given her time to write. Her mother had possessed some special gift for putting the boys to work and making them think they were playing. The fire sent out a small shower of sparks as the log broke in two, interrupting Bernadette's thoughts. She went to the kitchen to get something to drink.

In her mother's pantry, there was a rack of dusty bottles.

She chose a tall amber liquid with a homemade label. It said FORRIOR GERAUGH CURE. The first two words were Gaelic, and Bernadette didn't know what they meant. But *cure*? Was this medicine? It was in with the cordials. Her mother had always made her own liqueurs. (She had made her own everything.) Bernadette lifted the cork with effort and sniffed. It smelled of citrus and almonds; she took a swig. The taste was warm, like summer. She poured herself a short glass. My mother was a marvel, Bernadette thought.

She went over to the fire, glass in hand, driving a poker among the embers. The fire let out a small roar. It was mesmerizing. She felt a sudden urge to make a toast.

"Wish you were here, Mom," she said, lifting her glass to the fire and savoring a small sip. "And to youth—my last night of it."

The wind had picked up outside. Bernadette heard the trees rattle. Then, in a tremendous whoosh, the front door flew open. Leaves and dust blew inside on a whirlwind, which seemed to carry not only debris but sound, a hissing noise, like a swarm of bees. Bernadette rushed to the door to shut it, the liquid in her glass sloshing out when she hurriedly set it down.

Wasn't that door locked? she wondered. She was shaken by the violence of its sudden opening.

Almost as quickly, the air settled, and Bernadette felt inexplicably exhausted, far too tired to write. Rather automatically, she collected her bag and her laptop and climbed the stairs to the bedroom she had once shared with her sister, Claire.

PATRICK

TUESDAY, SEPTEMBER 8

Patrick woke up before his brothers and padded into the kitchen in his boxer shorts. He found the note Dad had left on the kitchen counter:

> P—
>
> *Mom spent the night at your grandmother's and my flight is at 6:30. If she's not back by the time you get up, please get Neil and Kevin off to school. Take $ for lunch from the envelope in the junk drawer if you need it. I should be home about 7 P.M.*
>
> *Thanks for your help. Knock 'em dead in seventh grade.*
>
> > Love,
> > Dad

"Where is everybody?" Neil said, rubbing the sleep out of his eyes as he entered the kitchen.

"We're on our own."

Neil opened a kitchen cabinet and pulled out a box of cereal.

"Can you get down a bowl?" he asked Patrick.

"Dad said to give you money for lunch," Patrick said, handing Neil a bowl.

"Yuck," Neil answered.

"Actually, Neil, the first day is usually not as bad as the rest of the year because even the cafeteria ladies are against serving leftovers from June."

"I am not eating that stuff. Chicken patties and carrot coins? It's not even really food." Neil tilted the open box and a shower of pink, purple, and green puffs fell into the bowl.

"Then what do you want?"

"Half a PB and J, a squeeze yogurt—the blue kind—a bag of potato sticks, nine grapes, and a juice box, but not cherry—fruit punch or apple. I don't like the cherry."

"So same as last year."

"Right."

Patrick crammed everything into Neil's lunch bag and his own, then went to rouse Kevin.

"Get up, Bun-Bun," he said, yanking off the covers and opening the blinds. Patrick knew that calling Kevin by the pet name his mother had for him would at least get his attention.

"Go away, *Tater*," Kevin answered. As an infant, Patrick's head supposedly had somewhat resembled a potato.

"Dad says you have to take Neil to his classroom."

"Where's Mom?" Kevin asked, putting the pillow over his head.

"She stayed at Grandma's. C'mon. Neil can't be late for the first day of second grade."

"You do it," Kevin said, sitting up. "I'm meeting Shane and Wade."

"Well, take Neil with you. You're going to the same place."

"No way. He walks too slow. And then he whines."

Patrick sighed. He couldn't care less if Kevin missed school, but his mother would kill him if Neil didn't get there on time. He would have to take him, even though it was the opposite direction from the middle school.

"You are useless," he told Kevin, rummaging through his drawer for a shirt he felt like wearing.

"Did you make me breakfast?"

"Wake up, Kevin." Patrick closed the drawer with a sharp push. "You're still dreaming."

"I feel a little sick," Neil said as they reached the elementary-school grounds.

Patrick glanced down at him. Oh, jeez. He did look pale.

"Neil—don't be nervous. This is second grade. It's the same as first grade only everybody's a little . . . bigger."

"I'm not nervous! I just don't feel so good anymore."

"Remember what Dad said? Give the teacher a chance. Don't listen to Bobby Yablonski. He eats dirt. How smart could he be?"

Neil looked unconvinced. Luckily, Mrs. Green was a pro, and she whisked Neil right off to show him his desk, waving over her shoulder at Patrick to let him know he could go. He ran back toward the middle school to catch up with Kyle and Duffy, but he could have walked because when he reached them, they were wrestling on someone's lawn.

Not that he would admit this to his friends, but Patrick actually enjoyed school, and not just because it was time away from his brothers. He was looking forward to chemistry and algebra, because science and math came easily to him.

The school lobby throbbed with kids and noise. Patrick had gotten his schedule in the mail over the summer, so he and Duffy knew they had two classes together and the same lunch period. But lockers were assigned alphabetically, so Kyle and Duffy stopped at theirs while Patrick kept walking down the seventh-grade corridor. He passed two guys from last year's basketball team who put out their hands for low fives. He had to part a sea of girls who were huddled right in front of his locker in order to put his things away.

The morning went quickly. Patrick's last class before lunch was band—his favorite subject. He had auditioned at the end of sixth grade for the jazz band and had made it. The jazz band director was a real musician who played in nightclubs on the weekends. He insisted the students call him Denny, not Mr. Grant.

"Mr. Grant is my father," he told them. Denny let them decide what songs the band would learn. "As long as it swings," he said.

That morning he had played them a Count Basie CD. They voted to learn "Jumpin' at the Woodside," and the music was still percolating through Patrick's head when he met Duffy at his locker to walk to the cafeteria.

Kyle was holding a place in the lunch line for them when they got there.

"Dudes," Kyle said. "Have you had your computer class yet?"

"No, we both have it eighth period," Patrick said. Even though he brought his lunch from home, Patrick always went through the food line with Duffy and Kyle. That way when he felt lazy about making his lunch each morning, he could easily remember what the alternative was.

"Get this—we all get e-mail," Kyle said.

"I'm okay with that," Duffy said.

"But make sure you get to class early," Kyle warned.

"Why?" Patrick asked.

"Because there are new computers, but only in the first three rows," Kyle explained.

"What's it going to be, son?" the cafeteria lady asked.

"Pizza," Kyle said, before turning back to Patrick and Duffy. "And my class was full, so a couple of people got stuck with the old machines." He took his tray. "Does that look like food to you?"

"No," Patrick said. The pizza was a square of red-and-orange congealed cheese. "What a hassle, though. You gotta race to get to computer class every day?"

"No. She assigns seats. Whatever seat you get today is the one you have for the rest of the year."

"Thanks for the 411, Kyle," Duffy said. "You are good for something."

Kyle punched Duffy in the arm. Duffy's tray shook and a few french fries fell. "Hey!" he called out.

"Sorry, bro. Want me to get those for you?"

Patrick sensed a wrestling match coming on, so he turned Duffy in the direction of an empty table.

"Let's get a seat, guys," he said.

Patrick got to eighth period a few minutes before Duffy did, so he snagged a seat in the second row and put his backpack on the seat next to him. But word about the new computers had apparently made the rounds. As the class started to fill up, a fistfight nearly broke out between two girls who both wanted the last seat in the row behind him. One of the girls was Victoria Cavendish, a snotty troublemaker who had been in Patrick's gym class last year. The other girl he didn't know, but she got the seat and Patrick thought, Good for you.

Kevin and Neil were already watching television by the time Patrick got home from school.

"Where's Mom?" he asked.

"Alien abduction," Kevin said.

"She hasn't been home?"

"Nope."

Because both his parents worked, Patrick was used to helping out with Neil, but by this time in the afternoon, his mother was usually home. And it *was* her birthday. Patrick had bought her a Mavericks CD. He figured that if she insisted on listening to country music, at least it could be *decent* country music.

"How was Mrs. Green?" he asked Neil.

"Great! She let me erase the boards," Neil said. "Hey—those grapes you gave me were squishy."

"Anytime you want to start making your own lunch is fine with me," Patrick said, dropping his backpack by the couch. He scrambled upstairs because he could sense Neil was thinking up a string of requests. He had to wrap the CD, too.

At five o'clock, his stomach grumbled. He tried his mother's direct line but got a recording. He hung up and redialed.

"City desk," a voice answered.

"Hi, this is Patrick McBride. I tried my mother's number, but I got her voice mail. Is she there?"

"No, honey. I haven't seen her all day. Want me to page her? Maybe she's out on a story," the woman volunteered.

"Okay," Patrick said. Moments later he heard the beeper go off—in the basket by the front door where his mother usually dumped it with her car keys when she came in. If she was out on a story, it was without her pager.

Patrick looked in the refrigerator because sometimes when his mother knew she would be late, she would make a casserole or a pasta salad ahead of time. But he didn't remember her doing that yesterday and he didn't see anything in there now that looked like dinner. So he made turkey sandwiches for himself and Neil, who complained because Patrick had put mayonnaise on only one slice of bread, not both. Patrick briefly considered turning the mayonnaise jar upside down on Neil's head but realized if he did, he would be the one that would have to clean it up.

Kevin ate an entire can of Pringles watching *Jerry Springer.*

Patrick was in the garage when he heard a car pull into the driveway. He put his guitar on its stand and went into the kitchen, expecting to see his mother. Instead it was Dad, carrying a supermarket cake and a bouquet of flowers.

"Where's Mom?" his father asked, setting the cake down on the counter.

"We haven't seen her," Patrick answered. "Didn't she call you?"

"I left my cell phone in the car when I got to the airport," he said. "Did you try the office?" he asked, picking up the telephone, punching in the numbers.

"I got voice mail, and the receptionist hadn't seen her. And her beeper's here."

His father hung up the phone.

"I just got her voice mail, too. Hmm, I wonder where she is . . ."

"Is that cake?" Neil asked, examining the box on the counter.

"Hey, buddy—how's my second grader?" Neil wrapped his arms around his father's waist. "Have you guys eaten?"

"Sort of . . ." Patrick answered.

"I'm going to drive over to your grandmother's," he said, patting Neil's back.

"But what about the cake, Dad?" Neil asked.

"We should wait for your mother," Dad said.

"But she wouldn't want us to waste food," Neil argued.

Uh-oh, thought Patrick. Here comes a rant. When it came to cake, Neil was not going to take later for an answer. He had seen Neil actually pant over frosting, following Mom around while she whipped butter and powdered sugar together, waiting to wrap his tongue around the goo clinging to the beater. Part of the problem was that his mother thought this was adorable. "Neil, you're my kind of boy," Patrick once heard her tell him.

"You want some, too?" his father asked Kevin, who had come into the kitchen.

"Sure," Kevin said.

"Dad, she probably wouldn't like this kind of cake anyway," Patrick said. His mother was fussy when it came to baked goods.

"I know, but the Cream Puff was closed," Dad said. "Okay, get some plates."

His father carved the cake into thick wedges. Neil polished off his first piece before Patrick had even taken a bite.

"Can I have one more slice?" Neil asked.

"Don't you think we should save a little for *Mom*?" Kevin said, and that held sway with even Neil. His father put the cross section of cake back in its flimsy cardboard home.

Patrick tried to eat his piece, but the frosting was sickly-sweet, and the cake tasted grainy and dry—nothing like the stuff his mother made. His favorite was this spicy applesauce cake she'd baked for his last birthday. It had smelled heavenly. But after he'd blown out the candles and cut the cake came the best part. She had drizzled warm caramel over each slice. Patrick had eaten two pieces on his birthday, then another slice for breakfast the next day.

When his father jumped to answer the phone, Patrick pushed his plate to Neil. Neil didn't eat the cake, but he used his finger to scrape off the icing.

"That was Mom's editor," Patrick's father said, hanging up the phone, "wondering why she hadn't heard from her all day." Patrick saw his father look at his watch. "Finish up, Neil," he said. Neil took a few more furious swipes at the icing. "Back to regular bedtime tonight."

"But it's not even eight o'clock!" Neil complained.

"Well, go upstairs and get your pajamas on. Do you have homework?"

"On the first day of school?" Neil asked.

"You, too, Kevin," his father said, clearing the plates from the table.

"What??? I don't have any homework and the Mets are on!" Kevin said.

"Are they? Well, get into your pajamas, then find out

what the score is." He turned to Patrick. "Will you finish up here and then get Neil to brush his teeth?"

"Yes, Dad," Patrick said. Why me? he was thinking.

"And read him a story, please?"

"You didn't ask *me* if I had homework."

"Do you?"

"Only if you count all this work I do at home."

"*Thank you,* Patrick."

"You're welcome, Dad."

Patrick was reading a book in bed when the door opened and Kevin came in.

"The Mets are in a rain delay," he said. "Are you staying up for a while?"

"Why?"

"I'm beat. Can we turn the lights off?"

"In a minute," Patrick said, since he was on the last page of a chapter. He finished it, marked his place, and put the book down. He had just turned out the light when he heard a sound from down the hall.

"Is that Neil crying?" Kevin asked.

"Sounds like it. Go see what's wrong," Patrick said.

"You do it. I'm already asleep."

Patrick threw back his covers and walked down the hall to Neil's room.

"What's up, Neil?" he asked, his eyes searching for his brother in the darkened room.

"My stomach hurts, Patrick." Neil was on the floor.

"You gonna hurl?"

"I think so."

"Well, get up. Don't do it in here," but even in the dark,

Patrick could see Neil looked green, so he picked him up and carried him to the bathroom. He knelt beside the toilet as Neil threw up. Patrick rubbed his back because that's what his mother had always done whenever he had been sick. Neil groaned and rested against the bathtub while Patrick went to get him clean pajamas.

"You want a glass of water?" Patrick asked him.

"I want Mommy," Neil said.

"Me, too."

When his father came through the front door, Patrick was sitting on the living-room couch. "Neil puked," he said.

"Was he upset about Mom?"

"Well, he asked for her, but I think it was all that cake that made him sick."

His father nodded. "I'll go check on him in a minute." Dad hung his coat on the rack in the hallway. "She wasn't there. The whole house was dark."

"Did you check inside? Maybe she was asleep."

"I don't have a key. *She* has the key. But I don't think anyone was there. I walked around the back, to see if I could look in the windows, but there weren't any lights on."

"Well, was her car there?"

"Yes, it was," his father said. Patrick thought he looked tired, and worried.

"Well, if her car's there, where else could she be?"

"I don't know, Patrick, but I'm sure there's some kind of explanation. Was yesterday just a bad day—I mean, were you three especially terrible?"

"I didn't think so. I mean, the computer ate her story and Neil kept bothering her and you forgot her birthday—"

"So, not a great day," Dad interrupted.

"Not great, but not bad enough to make her jump off a bridge. I mean, *definitely*, she's had worse days. A lot worse—like the time that Kevin found that smutty stuff on the Internet and invited half the neighborhood over, or the time that Neil Superglued his hand to the basketball—"

"Listen, get some sleep—I bet she'll be home by the time you wake up. My guess is another editor sent her out on a story and forgot to let anyone know. Or she's really mad at me for forgetting her birthday and she's making me pay."

"But how did she get anywhere without her car?"

"Maybe a photographer picked her up so they could go to the assignment together," he said. "I just don't know. Get some sleep, Patrick—and don't worry. Let me worry."

Patrick headed for the stairs.

"And Patrick," his father called after him. "Thanks for pitching in today."

"I'm gonna send you a bill."

"How about if I give you a day off?"

"How about a week?"

"Oooh, a whole week. That I'll have to discuss with your mother."

"Good night, Dad."

"Good night, Patrick."

BERNADETTE

TUESDAY, SEPTEMBER 8

On the morning of her fortieth birthday, Bernadette McBride woke up twelve again. It didn't dawn on her immediately. As the sun slanted across her narrow bed, what Bernadette first felt was the stiff cotton sheets drawn up under her chin. Sheets that had been starched and smelled of lavender.

Odd, she thought. Who starches sheets anymore?

"Bernadette!"

That sounds like my mother, she thought. *Oh, how I wish it were.* In her hazy state of half-waking, she tried to remember the last time she had heard her mother's lilting voice: Was it the day before she died? She had called on the telephone to ask Bernadette if she would drive her to the garden store.

"Are you up?" Another shout from downstairs.

That *is* my mother's voice, Bernadette thought. How could that be? She sat up and jerked her head around, searching for an explanation. White furniture with yellow trim. White shag carpeting. A poster of David Cassidy in a skimpy tank top, his muscled arms folded across his chest. Years ago, she had fought with her mother over putting it up. "Indecent," her mother had muttered.

Bernadette threw the covers back. She began to hyperventilate. I'm dreaming, she told herself, crossing to the mirror, an oblong piece of glass draped with strands of colored plastic beads. Tucked into the frame was a Polaroid of her and Linda Vesuvio, taken right before cheerleading tryouts, both of them wearing black leotards and wide smiles.

She saw her twelve-year-old self. The wispy brown hair. The fair skin. The flat chest. Braces! she thought, suppressing a gasp of horror. She had almost succeeded in forgetting she ever wore them.

She sat back down on the bed, the nubby chenille spread crumpling beneath her thin legs. Her mind furiously backtracked.

She had come to her mother's house the night before. She had sat in front of the fire, made a toast, shut the door after it opened in a fury of wind. Then she'd gone to bed.

And now here she was, shrunken but smooth, a small girl in a room where a woman had fallen asleep.

What is going on? Bernadette thought. Where are *my* kids? If I'm this young, do I even *have* kids? She laughed at that. Wow, the subconscious is powerful. My brain must have figured out the only way to get that assignment finished was inside a dream in which I have no children.

"Bernadette! You'll be late," her mother shouted.

Could her mother really be there, calling to her from the bottom of the stairs?

"Coming!" Bernadette answered. She had slept in a T-shirt that now fell almost to her knees.

She opened the closet. Her sister's side was empty, and Bernadette remembered it had taken her a few months after her sister left for college to spread her dresses and blouses to that side. That was the first year it was just she and her mother at home, the year she started seventh grade.

Was that what she was going to be late for? Seventh grade? Mercy! When she had joked to Gerard to make her younger, she was thinking twenty-five! Who in the world would want to be twelve again?

Bernadette did not understand how a dream could feel so real. Odd things *had* happened throughout her life, little things, and always when her mother was involved, but nothing like this. Once, a blackbird had flown into the house through an open window, and her mother called out in grief, "Oh, someone I love has died!" Her mother had explained the bird was a sure sign.

"But, Mom, if that were true, we could keep people alive forever just by putting up screens," Bernadette had said. That had made her mother laugh, which hadn't been Bernadette's intent.

"So very logical, Detta," her mother had answered, pulling her close with a hug.

A telegram had arrived a few hours later. Fiona's father in Ireland had passed away in his sleep. After that, Bernadette always thought twice before questioning her mother's superstitions.

Now Bernadette was in a desperate rush to get downstairs—before she woke up to find her mother gone again!

The clothes in the closet were uniformly ugly, but she chose a shirt and a pair of pants and threw them on her bed. She laughed when she found a bra in her underwear drawer—size 28AA.

First thing I'll do is tell my mother I love her. Bernadette felt sad all over again about never having had a chance to say good-bye. She pulled on a pair of kneesocks.

Also, I should ask her how she makes that stuff that cures coughs.

How much time do I have? she wondered. Would she have to be back to her real life by dinnertime in this dream? Tomorrow? The weekend? Was there time for ice-skating lessons? She buttoned the shirt, a polyester number with big blue-and-purple swirls. She remembered she had loved this shirt when it was new. Wow, did I have bad taste, she thought now, tucking it into a pair of equally hideous sailor-blue bell-bottoms.

She went back to the closet for shoes. Her laptop and overnight bag were still there. Should she bring them with her? No, she decided. Twelve-year-olds don't work, even in dreams. And it *is* my birthday, after all.

She took money out of her wallet thinking she wouldn't want to be caught without any cash—and then looked around for a place to stash her overnight bag and her laptop. She might have difficulty explaining to her mother why she had a laptop.

Bernadette remembered that she had loosened the screws on a heating vent years ago so she could stash her diary in the duct behind its metal grate. She wiggled the vent now, and it gave way. She wedged the laptop in first—it was a tight squeeze—and crushed the bag down on top of it. Then she fit the vent back into place.

She almost tumbled down the stairs in her rush but came to a full stop at the bottom step, peering into the kitchen, where her tiny mother was running water over something in the sink. Fiona's hair, which had gone brittle and gray in old age, had returned to its original color, glossy and black like the wing of a raven. Her skin was true white and smooth, like the shell of an egg.

Then Fiona turned and saw Bernadette, waiting on the stair.

"Happy birthday, lass," her mother said. "Breakfast is on the table."

Bernadette could not help but stare, fixing on her mother's most unusual feature—her bright eyes, one green, one blue. Bernadette's nose started to itch and her bottom lip quivered. Tears came to the rims of her eyes, so she took a deep breath to calm herself.

When she entered the kitchen, her mother was drying her hands on a dishtowel. She clamped Bernadette to her twiggish frame and kissed her forehead. "Your last year as a child. Next year, you'll be a teenager and incorrigible."

Bernadette was quiet, hoping the embrace would last longer than it did.

"Thank you, Mom. I love you," she said, squeezing her as tight as she could. "How *are* you?"

"Bernadette, you'll break me in two!" her mother said, and Bernadette relaxed her grip. Her mother looked at her quizzically. "I'm the same as always, of course," she said, and then, gesturing toward the table, "Go on. It's getting cold."

Bernadette ate deliberately. A bowl of oatmeal, a slice of soda bread with plump raisins, a cup of black tea. "Is there more bread?" she asked, licking marmalade from her finger.

"Why, Bernadette." Her mother paused. "It's good to see you hungry."

"It's good to see you," she replied.

Bernadette got another strange look from her mother when she hugged her around the middle and kissed her good-bye, but Bernadette wasn't sure what was going to happen next and didn't want any regrets. Then she grabbed the paper bag that held her lunch and darted for the front door.

"Bring a quart of milk, will you? I put the money in your sack," her mother called, a gray shadow behind the black mesh of the screen door.

"Okay," she called back, watching as her mother shut the door to the daylight. Throughout Bernadette's childhood, her mother had relied on her to fetch a pint of cream or a pound of butter and carry it home wedged between the books in her backpack.

When Bernadette reached the sidewalk, she realized that though *she* had been returned to her youth, the neighborhood had not. The man getting into a Ford Explorer next door wasn't her old neighbor, Mr. Cunningham. It was the man who had bought the house from the Cunninghams, a few years before. Across the street, there was a deluxe swing set in the yard where she and Linda Vesuvio had once splashed away every summer afternoon in an aboveground pool.

Bernadette walked toward Patrick's middle school. Her mind pumped faster than her legs. Could a dream feel this real? Were her children in this dream world, too? Would she see Patrick at school? Where was Gerard? Where was *she*?

Kids were moving in clumps toward the double doors. She tried to fall in behind one group, but she could see the girls giving her a quick up-and-down and then tightening their circles. Even with their heads turned, Bernadette could hear the stifled giggles. It was her clothes, she was sure—clothes that were too freaky for a new kid on the first day of school.

Her impulse was to leave—go where?—but then she saw Patrick, shuffling along with the Baxter twins. She forgot her discomfort about wearing bell-bottoms in a crowd of capri pants and watched him and his friends, uniformly dressed in oversized T-shirts, baggy jeans, and sneakers the size of gunboats, untied laces tracing trails in the dust.

What are Kevin and Neil wearing? she wondered. What did they eat for breakfast? Did Gerard remember to pack their lunches? She chuckled at the idea of Gerard having to take over for her for a day or two—that'd teach him to forget her birthday.

Patrick seemed to have survived a morning without her. He passed in front of her, and Bernadette had to restrain the urge to nudge a loose strand of his brown hair behind his ear. The bell rang and she hurried her steps inside.

In the lobby, teachers were inspecting slips of paper, pointing students off in different directions. Bernadette had nothing to show.

"Where's your schedule, young lady?" a tall woman in a yellow pantsuit asked.

"I'm new," she stammered.

"To Guidance, then. It's down that hall, on the right-hand side. What's your last name?"

Bernadette was struck dumb. Should she tell the woman her real name?

"Downey," she said. It was her father's name, *her* name before she married.

"A through G is Mrs. Piazza. She's on the left."

Bernadette needed time to think, so she was glad Mrs. Piazza had a line at her desk. She listened while Mrs. Piazza questioned the students in front of her, trying to figure out what information she was going to have to provide. But the other students were mostly making changes to their schedules. They weren't inventing new identities.

When Bernadette reached the front, Mrs. Piazza, a large woman whose bust was resting on her desk, was writing something in a file folder. "Next problem," she announced, without looking up.

"I don't have a schedule."

"Name," she barked, pulling closer a cardboard box full of envelopes that had been returned to the school by the post office.

"Detta Downey. You won't find me in that box, though. I'm new."

"New from where?"

"Ireland." She was guessing Mrs. Piazza wouldn't know enough about Ireland to ask specific questions Bernadette couldn't answer.

"Ireland? That's original. I don't suppose you have your school records with you."

"No . . . the school burned down."

"The school burned down?"

"Actually, the whole town burned down. That's why we moved here."

"I see. And you are living . . . ?"

"Twenty-four William Street."

"Have your parents been in here to register you?"

"No, there's only my mother and she doesn't drive."

"Doesn't drive? Also original. Well, that'll change. Everyone drives here," Mrs. Piazza said, standing to make a tight turn in her narrow cubicle, pulling open the top drawer of a tall file cabinet behind her. "How's your hand strength, Miss Downey?"

She didn't wait for an answer. "All these forms will give you pencil cramps," she said, shuffling through folder after folder, extracting a sheet from each one.

She turned, resting one hand on her wide hip, looking at Bernadette over purple bifocals. "What kind of student are you, Detta?"

"A's and B's."

"Do you have old report cards you could bring in so we could see what subjects you've taken?"

"No, ma'am. Nothing like that. You get promoted or you don't."

"Not big on paperwork, huh? Boy, I know teachers here who would like that system." Mrs. Piazza pushed the file drawer shut. "Well, without school records, we'll have to test you. How about a birth certificate? Surely they have those."

"Yes, ma'am." Mrs. Piazza wiggled herself back into her chair. Bernadette thought Mrs. Piazza wouldn't be half as cranky if she had more space.

"Okay, complete Form 360A and attach a birth certificate. It has to be signed by a parent. What about vaccinations?" Again, Mrs. Piazza didn't seem interested in an answer. "You need proof you've been inoculated against measles, mumps, rubella, smallpox, tetanus, whooping cough, tuberculosis, polio, diphtheria, and hepatitis B—it's all here, Form 144. Unless you want to be jabbed a bunch of times, I'd try to come up with the records."

"Okay."

"Student handbook—read that," she said, the book thudding into Bernadette's outstretched arms, "and sign the last page.

"Internet privacy form. Read it, sign it. Antidrug pledge. Read, sign. Dress code. I'll hit the highlights. No bellybuttons, Miss Downey, we do all our navel gazing in the privacy of our own homes here in the USA. And skirts have to be 'fingertip length,' which means—put your arms straight down at your sides, Detta."

Bernadette laid the stack of forms on Mrs. Piazza's desk and dropped her arms.

"Skirts have to be longer than where your fingers reach on your thigh. Got that?"

Bernadette nodded.

"No pierced appendages, other than earlobes. Hair must be a color found in nature. There's more, but those are the biggies. Read the whole thing. . . ."

"And sign it." Bernadette took the booklet and added it to her stack.

Mrs. Piazza laughed. "You catch on quick. Oh—are you an alien?"

"Excuse me?"

"Are you here legally on a visa?"

"No, I was born here. We were in Ireland for . . . a while."

"Hallelujah! So you have a Social Security number? That would help because there's another raft of forms for aliens. I noticed you don't have much of a brogue."

"I'll ask my mother about the Social Security number," Bernadette said.

"Start filling out these forms while I get the placement tests. I hope you didn't have your heart set on starting chemistry today, because this will take you all morning," Mrs. Piazza gestured to a conference table. "Move over there with your bag. Is this all you have?" she asked, holding up Bernadette's crumpled brown bag. "No backpack? No roll-aboard luggage? That'll change, too."

Bernadette was happy to be left alone with her forms. She was going to have to mesh the lies she told with the facts of her new existence. Name, address—she stopped cold at *Date of birth*.

I'm twelve, she thought to herself, backtracking through the years to create a new birth date. Time for some creative writing, she thought.

Mrs. Piazza was heaving great sighs at each new problem to arrive at her desk, but after forty-five minutes, the office cleared out. Bernadette had worked deliberately, thinking carefully about each blank space. She had just finished the forms when she heard the bell ring for the first class change.

Mrs. Piazza had emerged from her cubicle to refill her coffee cup. She had a pencil behind one ear and an ID badge on a lanyard around her neck. Her bifocals were nesting in her blond bouffant. Bernadette found herself thinking they were probably the same age. They probably shopped at the same grocery store.

"Detta Downey! My, you Irish girls are quiet. Have you finished those forms?" Mrs. Piazza seemed friendlier now that the crush had ended.

"Yes, ma'am."

"Quiet *and* polite," Mrs. Piazza said. "More things likely to change. Let's do the placement tests, then. Do you need water or the girls' room?"

"No, I'm fine."

There was a test in math, social studies, reading comprehension, science, and English composition, and for the first time in her life, Bernadette found test-taking enjoyable. The math was like a game: calculate the median price of three tubes of toothpaste; find a percentage for a tip on a lunch bill.

She chuckled at the "history" questions, which included events that had occurred during her own lifetime: *Name the California governor who became the oldest man elected to the U.S. presidency.* Heck, I *voted* in that election, Bernadette thought as she penciled in Ronald Reagan's name. The tests were a lot easier than the forms.

"All done?" Mrs. Piazza asked. Bernadette was standing at her desk again, the stack of papers in her hand. "It's going to take some time to grade these and put together a schedule. You Irish girls do eat, right? I'll send you to the cafeteria."

Mrs. Piazza squeezed out from behind her desk and walked to the door, her head scanning both ends of the hallway. "Donna Feinman," she called, gesturing for someone to come to the office.

A tall, thin girl with a mane of brown corkscrew curls appeared in the doorway. She gave Mrs. Piazza a mock salute.

"Donna, this is Detta Downey. Detta, this is Donna. Nobody named David better show up, right?" Mrs. Piazza laughed at her own joke. Donna rolled her eyes.

"Donna, please take Detta to the cafeteria and introduce her around. She's new, not only to us, but also to America."

Donna smiled and stuck out her hand. "Detta? Is that short for something?"

"Yes, but I go by Detta."

They turned left down the hallway. "Where are you from?" Donna asked.

"Well, I'm from here, but I had been living in Ireland for a while."

"Like U2."

"Right," Bernadette said, furiously trying to think of the name of a U2 song, in case Donna pursued the topic. Luckily, she didn't.

"Those are some phat threads, Detta," Donna said. "Are they vintage?"

"Yes," said Bernadette, unable to suppress a smile. "They're vintage."

"You will have to share the secrets of the Irish educational system," Mrs. Piazza said when Bernadette returned from the cafeteria. "I've never had anybody deliver a perfect score on all five placement tests before. You sure you're twelve?"

The only thing I'm sure of, Bernadette found herself thinking, is that there won't be anyone to make dinner for the boys tonight. While she was sitting in the cafeteria, she had remembered that Gerard was out of town and wouldn't be home until early evening. She wished she could somehow tell Patrick to make sandwiches for his brothers, but she hadn't seen him since the morning. Also, what would she say?

"Excuse me, I may not seem familiar to you, but your mother wants you to get dinner on the table for your brothers tonight. Don't let Kevin eat junk. See you later. I hope."

But probably I'll be back to normal by dinnertime, she reminded herself. I'm worrying about nothing.

"Detta? Still with me?" Mrs. Piazza was fanning the air in front of Bernadette's face with a piece of paper. "Let me show you what I've come up with for your schedule."

"Sorry." Bernadette sat in the plastic chair Mrs. Piazza held out and looked at the paper placed in front of her. Language Arts, PE, Social Studies, Lunch, Algebra, Chemistry, Study Hall, and finally, a class called Computer Literacy.

I cannot escape that darn computer, Bernadette thought.

"I gave you a study hall, but if you want more to do, there's band seventh period—do you play an instrument?"

Would they give her a guitar? Bernadette wondered. "I don't play anything, but I'd like to try," she said.

"Done. We'll put you in band instead." Mrs. Piazza used her eraser to make the change. "Now, if you hurry, you'll make it to fifth period. That's math with Mrs. Fermat. Room 216. Take the steps at the opposite end of this hallway. It's the third door on the right upstairs."

"Thanks, Mrs. Piazza."

"My pleasure. Now, these are the forms your mother needs to sign, and I wrote down everything you're missing on this yellow sticky," she said, handing Bernadette a folder.

"Be advised. If you don't turn them in, I will hunt you down like a dog."

The afternoon passed uneventfully. Bernadette was new but so were a lot of other people. Mrs. Fermat issued textbooks and went over her grading system. The chemistry teacher talked with enthusiasm about the combustible nature of common household cleaning products. In band, Bernadette chose a flute from a closet full of used instruments. Because her brain was tired, she was glad her last class was Computer Literacy, a topic she felt sure she already knew enough about.

The computer lab was crowded and Bernadette was scanning the tables for an empty terminal when she saw Patrick, in the second row, his eyes fixed on the monitor, his right hand moving the mouse around.

"Good afternoon. If everybody will find an empty terminal, we'll get started." The teacher's name, according to Bernadette's schedule, was Dobbs. The seats on either side of Patrick were taken, but there was an empty terminal behind him, and Bernadette made a beeline for it. She saw another girl making her way toward the same seat from the other direction. She nearly ran to reach it first.

"That seat is saved," said a blond girl at the next terminal as Bernadette tried to slip into the chair. The blond's hand grasped the chair at the same moment Bernadette's did. Bernadette pretended she hadn't heard her and sat down.

"I *said* that seat is saved," the girl repeated. Bernadette glared at her.

"Ladies, what's the trouble?" Ms. Dobbs asked. The friend, a brunette who was wearing the same beaded choker as the blond, grunted in disgust and walked to an empty seat in the next row.

"Bitch," the blond girl said with a snarl. Bernadette had to restrain herself from slapping this girl soundly across the face. How dare she speak to me like that! she thought.

"Welcome to Computer Literacy," Ms. Dobbs said. "I know you're all dying to turn the computers on, but first I want you to fill out this survey so I can get an idea of how much you already know about computers."

Bernadette looked at the form and sighed quietly, thinking about the additional lies she was going to have to tell.

"When you've completed the form, hand it to the front. Today we'll turn on the computers and begin the process of learning our way around the desktop. Whatever seat you are in now will be your assigned seat for the rest of the term, so you won't have to redo the settings every time you come to class."

Yes! thought Bernadette. She had already wondered if she would have to fight the blond's friend every day for the seat near Patrick.

"When do we get e-mail?" It was the blond on Bernadette's left.

"This first week, everybody introduce yourself when you have a question, so I learn your names. Your name is?" Ms. Dobbs asked.

"Victoria Cavendish." Bernadette gave her the up-and-down. She certainly had style. Black ribbed sweater with fake-fur collar and cuffs. Black jeans and sparkly, silver platform sneakers.

"Victoria . . . oh, here you are," Ms. Dobbs said, looking over her roster. She made a check mark. "Victoria, we will set up e-mail accounts, but not today. That'll come later this week."

"What are you looking at?" Victoria growled, catching Bernadette's glance. "Keep your eyes on your own ugly self."

Bernadette's head snapped around to the front. Maybe a study hall *this* period would be a good idea. But then she'd miss an opportunity to check up on Patrick. The computers were on long tables, and the slight stagger of their alignment meant Bernadette could see the back of his head and his screen. It wasn't much, but it was a small way to stay connected to him. She couldn't let this witch prevent that.

And it was too bad they weren't getting e-mail today, she thought.

She could have sent Patrick a message about dinner.

Patrick

WEDNESDAY, SEPTEMBER 9

Wednesday morning, Patrick woke to the sound of a car door slamming outside his bedroom window. That must be Mom, he thought.

But when he bent the blinds to peer out at the street, he saw Mr. Yablonski, across the street, carrying a box of doughnuts up the front walk.

In the kitchen, Patrick's father had the telephone wedged between his shoulder and his ear while he poured coffee.

"Is that the hospital?" Patrick asked, expecting his father would soon be hurrying off, leaving Patrick to get Neil to school again.

"Sheriff's department," his father said. "I'm on hold."

Patrick opened the refrigerator, though as soon as he did, he realized he wasn't hungry. Now the police were involved. Where *was* his mother?

"Hand me the cream, Patrick," his father asked. "Yes, I'm here," his father said into the phone, straightening up.

Patrick poured cream into his father's coffee and got a spoon from the drawer while he listened to his father's side of the conversation.

"Monday night . . .

"No, her car is still there . . .

"I don't have a key, but from the outside, it looks unoccupied."

Patrick heard his father give his grandmother's address before hanging up.

"Patrick, can you take Neil to school? I'm going to meet them at your grandmother's," Dad said, blowing steam from the top of his cup.

"Sure," Patrick said.

"I'm going to take a quick shower," his father said.

"Okay."

"Patrick—you look worried."

"I *am* worried. Where could she be?"

"Hopefully, she's taking the snooze of her life. She *has* been tired," he said. "But listen: Don't say anything about the sheriff to Neil or Kevin. Just tell them I had to run out if they ask."

Patrick made lunches, woke Neil, and got out some clothes for him to wear. He practically dragged him to school.

"Are we late?" Neil asked him.

"No, we're fine."

"Well, then, why are we running?"

"Oh. I'm just excited about getting to school myself," Patrick said. "I'll slow down."

"When is Mom going to be home?"

"Soon," Patrick told him, hoping that was true.

"This is too much walking," Neil said, stopping on the sidewalk. "My legs hurt."

I'm not carrying him, that's for sure, Patrick thought, before hitting upon the solution. "I'll race you the rest of the way."

"Okay! Do I get a head start?" Neil asked.

"You bet. Ready?"

"Ready!"

"Go!" Patrick watched as Neil sprinted off. He waited until his brother was half a block ahead, then he picked up his pace to a jog.

After he got Neil to his classroom, Patrick hurried to his grandmother's. He had considered asking his father if he could meet him there, but his father would have said no. Better to just do it than ask and be told no, Patrick decided.

But by the time he reached William Street, the only car Patrick recognized was his mother's, parked in the driveway of his grandmother's house. The sheriff and his father were already gone.

And now he was late for school himself. He thought about going home, to see if his father was there, but school was closer and Neil was right—they had been doing a lot of walking.

School *almost* took his mind off his mother—at lunch, he realized he had forgotten about the sheriff during his last class. And the longer the day wore on, the easier it was to convince himself that the police hadn't found anything at his grandmother's. If they had found something bad, Patrick knew his father would have come to pick him up.

When he got home that afternoon, his father was in the kitchen again, talking on the telephone. Patrick put his book bag on a chair. On the table there were empty cups and plates—evidence that Kevin and Neil had already had an after-school snack. Patrick cleared the table so he could continue to eavesdrop. It sounded like his father was talking to his office, rescheduling appointments.

"Hey," his father said, hanging up the phone.

"What happened?"

"What happened with what?"

"With the sheriff?"

"Nothing happened. They forced open the door, but she wasn't there. And her things weren't there. There was an empty glass that maybe she drank out of—by the fireplace—but that was it."

"Well, where'd she go without a car?"

"I don't know. Listen, I need you to go upstairs and keep Neil busy. I sent him to change his clothes, but stall him. I'm going to call Aunt Claire and your uncles."

"Dad, can I stay home tomorrow," Patrick asked him, "to help you look?"

"I'm not looking, Patrick. I'm waiting," his father answered.

Saturday morning, Patrick normally would have slept in, but he wasn't sleeping well, much less sleeping late. None of them were. By the time he got up for breakfast, his brothers were already in the kitchen. Kevin was at the table, reading the cornflakes box intently, as if there would be a quiz on it come Monday.

"Figured out what riboflavin is yet?" Patrick asked. Kevin glanced up, briefly, before returning to the box.

Neil had his crayons out. "How do you spell 'lost'?" he wanted to know.

"L-O-S-T," Patrick told him as he put a waffle in the toaster.

His father ambled in, looking bad, smelling sour. If Mom were here, Patrick thought, she would tell him he needs a shower.

"Is this the right phone number?" Neil asked, holding up the paper he'd been writing on. Patrick's father squinted to read LOST MOM, written in red scrawl, with the phone number beneath it. His face sank. Patrick's waffle popped, startling him.

"Neil, buddy, whatcha doing?" his father asked.

"I'm making posters so if somebody finds Mom, they'll know we're looking for her. When Snowflake was lost, the Yablonskis put up posters and they got Snowflake back."

Patrick saw his father eye the empty coffeepot, then cross the room to put his hand on Neil's head. "That's a good idea, Neil. You keep making them, and I'll put them up myself later."

"No, I want to put them up now."

Patrick could see a tantrum starting to form like a storm gathering behind dark clouds. From across the room, Patrick willed his father to say yes.

"Okay. Let me get coffee." Patrick thought his father looked like he might cry. "Patrick, when you're done with your breakfast, please get the staple gun from the garage and then we'll go."

At lunch, Patrick was pouring milk into four tall glasses when his father offered a theory: Mom needed a break.

"You mean she's having a midlife crisis?" Kevin asked.

Patrick put the milk back in the refrigerator, then took his seat at the table.

"What's a midlife crisis?" Neil wanted to know.

"This happened to George on *Seinfeld*," Kevin offered. "He got a toupee."

Patrick flashed Kevin a look that said, *You're not helping.* His father ignored Kevin and looked directly at Neil.

"What I mean is that sometimes, when you get older, you think about the choices you've made and you wonder if you've made the right ones," he explained. "And I think with Grandma gone, your mother had been worrying about things she didn't say, or do, and I think her job wore her out this summer and . . ."

Patrick listened but found himself wondering what this had to do with him, or his father, or his brothers. He understood his mother being sad about Grandma. He missed her, too, though he hadn't admitted it to anyone. But even his mother had said thank God she had her boys, that they gave her so much to do she didn't have time to be sad. He had heard her say that a couple of times, to people who called on the telephone. They still gave her as much to do, didn't they? What with school starting and soccer tryouts? How would leaving help?

"And, really, guys, I blew it big-time by forgetting her birthday," Dad said. "I think this is all my fault."

"So what does that mean?" Patrick asked.

"What does what mean?" his father answered.

"A 'break.' "

"Well, I think—I *hope*—she's taking a little time for herself to sort things out."

"Like a vacation?" Neil asked.

"Exactly," Dad said.

Patrick didn't say anything, but he considered this very unlikely. He glanced up at Kevin, who looked at him and rolled his eyes.

Okay, so Kevin's not buying this either, Patrick thought.

Sunday night, Patrick helped his father make dinner.

"There isn't any good in me staying home next week," his father said, and Patrick had to agree. When he was home, all Patrick could think of was that his mother wasn't. Her absence hung like a stale smell over the house. Kevin was his usual catatonic self, but Neil had been whining more than ever. He quickly tired of the dinners his father made—hot dogs, scrambled eggs, and, tonight, macaroni and cheese out of a box.

"Why can't we have lasagna?" Neil asked, when they were all seated at the table. "Mom always makes lasagna on Sunday."

"Not always, Neil, and this has the same stuff as lasagna—pasta and cheese," Dad said. "I can't make lasagna. There are all these . . . steps."

"I don't like orange cheese. I like white cheese," Neil said.

"We'll go out and get lasagna, okay?" Patrick noticed his father was offering a lot of bribes these days.

"You could at least try it, Neil," Patrick encouraged him, but Neil pushed his plate forward.

Patrick scratched at some crud, baked onto the edge of his plate.

"Who set the table?" he asked.

"I did," Kevin said. "Even though it was *Neil's* turn."

"Where'd you get these plates?"

"Out of the dishwasher," Kevin said.

"Were they clean?" Patrick asked.

"They were in the dishwasher."

"Yeah, but had anybody turned the dishwasher on?"

"Yuck! Look at the bottom of mine—this is spaghetti sauce from last night," Neil said, tipping his plate forward. Some of the macaroni and cheese slid off the plate and onto the table. "Gross. I'm not eating off this."

"Hey—I just wiped down the table!" Kevin shouted. "Watch it!"

"Time out!" Dad said. "Let's not yell."

After dinner, Patrick's father told him and Kevin to go sit in the living room. Then he put on a video for Neil in the family room.

"I'm going to need you boys to pick up the slack around here," he said, lowering himself onto the couch. He started listing chores. Patrick's mother hadn't even been gone a week, but every room in the house revealed evidence of her absence. The beds didn't get made and the laundry had reached mountainous levels.

Patrick listened to his father, thinking, This means more work for me. Kevin artfully avoided chores with his selective deafness, tuning out things it wasn't in his interest to hear, usually by turning up the volume on the TV.

"We need to do one load of laundry every day," his father said, "before the TV goes on, Kevin."

"I don't know how to do laundry."

"Well, you'll learn. It's not any harder than programming a VCR. We also need to keep a grocery list."

"I'll do that," Kevin said.

"No way," Patrick objected. "We'll die of malnutrition."

His father continued. Saturday mornings, one could do tops, which was Patrick's mother's word for dusting, and the other bottoms, which was vacuuming and mopping. The next week they'd swap.

"But soccer starts this Saturday," Kevin said.

"Well, you'll have to do your chores before soccer."

"Is Mom still going to be on vacation next Saturday?" Patrick asked. His father gave him a long look.

"I don't know," his father answered. "I hope not."

After Neil went to bed, Patrick's father told him, "You're in charge," and left the house. He had a screwdriver with him, and Patrick guessed that he was going to take down Neil's posters. When his father came back half an hour later, he pushed open Patrick's bedroom door.

"Everything all right?"

Patrick knew he meant since he went out, but he wanted an answer to a different question. "No, Dad, it isn't."

"Your mother will be back, Patrick."

"What if she's dead?"

His father winced, so Patrick knew he had wondered the same thing.

"She isn't dead, Patrick. I'm sure she just needed a break."

Deep down, Patrick believed this, that his mother was alive, somewhere. But where was she waking up each morning, without them? How could a school day start without her sending at least one of them back to his room to make another choice about what to wear? There were no lunches in paper bags. No afternoon interrogations about homework.

His father sat down on Patrick's bed, his lean frame barely depressing the mattress. Patrick looked at him, memorizing his face, trying to recall his mother when she had last stood at the threshold of his room. She had the gym bag slung over one shoulder. She was wearing the red sweater she bought for the family Christmas photo last year. They had all worn matching red sweaters, and Patrick remembered telling her, angrily, that he was too old for matching sweaters.

Now Patrick studied his father's profile, the furrows in his brow and the faint, crisscrossed lines around his eyes. His father must have forgotten the roll of posters in his back pocket, because as soon as he sat down on Patrick's bed, he lifted himself up again to yank them out.

"I took down all of these, except the one on the telephone pole right out front," he said. "We'll have to be careful not to drive past places where Neil will notice they're gone." He pulled the papers at one end to tighten the coil.

"Dad, can you do me a favor?"

"Sure, Patrick."

"Tomorrow, can we call the police in Nashville?"

BERNADETTE

That first day, Bernadette stopped at the grocery store on her way home from school. From the black tea and the unbuttered bread, she could tell her mother had fashioned breakfast from her store of dry goods. So Bernadette bought milk, like her mother asked, but also butter, bananas, apples, sliced turkey from the deli counter, and a package of Swiss cheese. Then she headed for the bakery.

The tall brown bag nearly covered her face, but she peered past her reflection in the bakery window to see who was behind the counter. Agnes. Good. She was fairly new. She wouldn't recognize Bernadette as a twelve-year-old.

She pushed the door open with her hip. She inhaled deeply, the warm, sweet smell flooding her with memories of working at the Cream Puff in high school. She thought about her first job, as a decorator, working at a long aluminum table in the back. She'd dip cookies into melted chocolate, lay them on waxed paper, and scatter handfuls of chopped nuts or colored sprinkles over the tray. She'd mix butter, sugar, and food coloring into a canvas funnel and squeeze swirls and curlicues and roses onto layer cakes.

"What'll it be, sweetie?" Agnes asked.

"Is there any seven-grain bread left?"

"Lemme see," she said, turning to look at the rack. "It's your lucky day. I got one loaf. You want it sliced?"

"No, thanks."

Agnes slotted the bread into a white paper bag. "Anything else?"

"How about one of those napoleons for my mother?" Bernadette asked, pointing at a tray inside a glass case.

"What a good daughter! How 'bout I throw in a few cookies for you, too?"

"Sure. Thank you," Bernadette said, thinking about the profits the Cream Puff had lost over the years giving out cookies to kids. When Kevin and Patrick were little, they'd get shortbread sandwich cookies with raspberry filling and sugar-dusted tops that left circles of white powder around their mouths. Her favorite part was watching them eat, and drinking in the smell of the bakery. When she worked there, Bernadette got so used to the scent of baking bread she didn't notice it anymore. She would leave on her break to get a sandwich from the deli and feel intoxicated by the aroma when she returned.

When she thought about it now, that was her only regret about her years at the Cream Puff. All those hours she'd spent there, not being able to smell the smell.

And it was that living, real, familiar smell that now woke up the rest of her senses. This isn't a dream I'm in, she realized with certainty. You don't dream smells like this. It's something else. Something that's never happened to me before.

"Four twenty-five, honey," Agnes said, knotting the red-and-white twine around the small white box that held the napoleon and the cookies.

Bernadette paid her. Then she tucked the bread and the box into the larger grocery bag.

She had planned to walk past her house on Jackson Avenue so she might catch a glimpse of Kevin and Neil, but her purchases weighed her down, so she went straight to her mother's. Tomorrow, she thought. *If* I'm still twelve.

"Mom?" she called out, pushing the kitchen door open.

"I'm going to sit right down and write myself a letter. And make believe it came from you. . . ."

She could hear her mother's high-pitched warbling from the laundry room. Bernadette couldn't help but laugh. Her mother was a terrible singer. Bernadette remembered how it used to drive her crazy. It was so . . . embarrassing.

"Here's the milk. I bought a few other things, too."

The kettle was in full screech when her mother materialized. "Turn it off, will you?" she said, nodding to the stove. Drops of water spurted out, dancing on the hot burner. "How was school?"

"Interesting," Bernadette said, practically the first true thing she had said all day. "I brought you a napoleon."

"Bread, too?" her mother said, poking her nose into the bag. "Mmm. The staff of life."

Bernadette felt warmed by being able to make her mother happy. She left her in the kitchen, slicing bread, humming.

The computer class had made her think of her laptop. She could use it to get word from—what would she call it? Her past? Her previous life? Her future? What kind of message could she send that would let her family know she was okay? *Was* she okay? She just didn't want them to worry.

She jiggled the vent cover and removed the bag and the laptop. She flipped the laptop open and hit the power button. Nothing. This stupid machine. She had gotten a new battery two weeks before. It couldn't be dead already.

She pulled the power cord from its slot in the carrying case and plugged it into the back of the laptop. She moved Claire's bed away from the wall to reach the electrical outlet. The machine still didn't work. She hit the power button a few more times, but the screen stayed dark. She stashed it back in the heating duct with her overnight bag and fixed the cover back in place. Rats, she thought.

She plopped down on her bed and looked out the window at the thick stand of oaks in the woods behind her home. When she was a girl, she had looked intently out this window often, hoping to see the fairies from her mother's stories. Her mother believed in fairies, said if you knew where to look for them, you could find them drinking water from the upturned bells of flowers.

She remembered a legend her mother told about a woman spirited away to nurse the baby of the fairy queen, who had been cursed by an enemy of Fin Varra, the fairy king. In Fiona's stories, people were routinely stolen by fairies—grooms on their way to the altar, babies right from the cradle, women with special talents, like fiddle playing or step dancing.

"One was always hearing about neighbors who'd been seen in Fin Varra's court, trying to send messages to their families to be no ways uneasy about them," her mother would tell her.

Did the fairies get me? Bernadette wondered. How do I get back?

She had other, more immediate worries, too. She walked halfway down the stairs and peeked around the banister. She could see her mother in a chair by the fire, her sewing basket at her feet. Bernadette padded back upstairs and into her mother's room, holding her breath as she slid back the closet door. From the top of the closet, she took down a cardboard box with her name written on it in black marker.

Inside, she found a copy of her birth certificate, old report cards, and a picture frame made of macaroni with a photograph of Bernadette at age six. There was an amateurish watercolor painting of the lilac hedge in the backyard. No wonder I became a writer, she thought. There was no Social Security card or medical records. Of course not, she realized. They're at *my* house. She took the birth certificate and put the box back.

In her room, she used a fine-tip black pen to change her birth date from 1960 to 1988, closing the top loop in the six and dividing the zero in half. She looked at it appraisingly. The only chance she had to pass it off as real was to make a photocopy of it, rather than giving Mrs. Piazza the original. She put it under her bed where her mother wouldn't see it if she came in the room.

Then Bernadette climbed into bed for a nap, exhausted but anxious about falling asleep, wondering who she'd be when she woke up.

PATRICK

The second week of school began with Neil in tears, crying over his cereal bowl because he didn't like the breakfast choices.

"Neil, what can I do?" Patrick asked him, pleading. "We're out of the kind you like." Dad had gone to the grocery store over the weekend, but Patrick now realized he shouldn't have let him go alone—he hadn't bought the right stuff.

"I can't eat this," Neil said, and he began to sob.

"What's with him?" Kevin asked, coming into the kitchen.

"He doesn't like the cereal," Patrick said. Neil was howling.

"Epic meltdown," Kevin said. Just then Dad came in. He looked at Patrick for an explanation. "Wrong cereal," Patrick told him. His father scooped up Neil and took him out of the room.

"Think this could have something to do with Mom being on 'vacation'?" Kevin asked.

"Cut the sarcasm, Kevin, okay?" Patrick said. He had lost his appetite, too.

Luckily for Patrick, his father told him he'd drive Kevin and Neil to school, so Patrick was finally able to walk to his own school with Kyle and Duffy. He was anxious to get away from the house. He wanted to pretend everything was normal.

But it wasn't. And Patrick sensed that other people knew something was up. He felt their stares. He heard them whispering, but going quiet when he looked their way.

At lunch, he asked Duffy, "Is there something weird about the way I look?"

"No, man. Why?"

"People are giving me funny looks."

Duffy was spelling out curse words with his french fries. He had written H-E-L-L, but was now trying to make a fry curve into a D, to go along with the A-M-N he had already arranged on his tray. "No, you look fine."

"Then what is it? Look," Patrick said, nodding toward a table of girls. "No, now they looked away. They were all staring at me."

"They *want* you," said Kyle.

"Yeah, right." Patrick took another bite of his burger.

When Patrick got to Language Arts after lunch, Mrs. Christie gestured for him to come to her desk.

"I am so sorry about your mother," she said in a conspiratorial whisper. "Have you heard anything?"

Patrick was taken aback by her question. He wondered how she knew about his mother. Then he realized *everybody* knew. That explained the stares and whispers.

"No, we haven't," he said.

"Please let me know if there's anything I can do . . . if you need someone to talk to," she said.

"Okay, thanks," Patrick said, certain he would never take her up on her offer. He trudged down the aisle to his seat, looking at Duffy.

"Do you know about my mother?" he whispered.

Duffy nodded. "It was in the newspaper."

"Why didn't you tell me?"

"You didn't know your mother was missing?"

"No, you jerk. Why didn't you say something about it being in the paper?"

"Well, I thought you knew. I mean, your mother *works* for the paper."

"Yeah, but she's not working if she's missing, right?"

"Well, yeah, but I didn't bring it up because I thought you didn't want to talk about it." Duffy pretended to be looking in his backpack for something. Mrs. Christie was resting her bottom against the front of her desk with a book open in her hands, waiting for the rustle of belongings to die down.

"What did the story say?"

"It said she was missing."

"What else?"

"Mr. McBride, Mr. Baxter, we're about to begin," Mrs. Christie cut in.

Patrick and Duffy looked down at their books. Mrs. Christie started her lecture, which was on Edgar Allan Poe.

Normally, Patrick would have given Mrs. Christie his full attention because he was interested in what she had to say. She had a reputation as a tough grader, but she was a nut for detective stories and mysteries.

Patrick scribbled, *What else?* on a clean sheet in his notebook and held it up at a slight angle so Duffy could read it. Duffy gave him a vacant stare, then scribbled back:

What else what?

Boy, Duffy could be dense.

What else did the story say? Patrick wrote. Mrs. Christie was talking about Poe getting kicked out of the University of Virginia and being broke most of his life.

The cops don't think anything bad happened to her.

Patrick drew in his breath in relief. Then he scrawled: *When was this?*

Duffy scrunched his eyes together in a quizzical look. Patrick wrote: *The story. When did it run?*

Duffy looked deep in thought. *Yesterday. No, Saturday,* he wrote.

Patrick wondered if his father had deliberately hidden the newspaper from them.

"She's not missing," Patrick whispered to Duffy. "She's taking a break."

"Sure, I know," Duffy whispered back. "My father always says you can't believe what you read in the newspaper."

After Language Arts, Patrick went directly to the school library, which was in a portable classroom near the basketball courts. It had started to rain midmorning, and it didn't take a lot of water to flood the walkways to the portables, which had been strategically located in some kind of swamp. He would get in trouble for being late to sixth period, probably get a detention, but he didn't care. What would they do, he thought, call his mother?

The library was almost empty. Patrick knew who the librarian was but hadn't had much to do with her last year. Now he saw the nameplate on her desk, which read MRS. FITZJAMES, and he realized why she had always seemed familiar to him. She taught catechism at his church. She had been Kevin's teacher once, and Patrick remembered Kevin had liked her, which was saying something, because Kevin was not fond of church. Patrick wiped his wet shoes on the mat before crossing the carpet to her desk.

"Ma'am, do you have back issues of newspapers here?"

"A few. They're over there behind the computer stations. We keep *Newsday* and the *Farmingdale Observer* for a couple of weeks, until we run out of shelf space. Will that do you?"

"I think so," Patrick said.

"You can help yourself, but if you take them out of order, put them back the way you found them. I don't have an aide this year." Mrs. Fitzjames stood up and pushed back her chair. "Do you have a pass to be in here?" she asked.

"I forgot to get one from study hall," Patrick lied.

"Well, bring me one later. You'll probably get stopped on the way back and sent to the office, though," she warned. "Excuse me while I work on my inventory, such as it is." She turned her back and walked toward a short stack of cardboard boxes. "I'll be over here if you need help."

Patrick crossed to the other side of the room and put his backpack on a wooden table.

The most recent newspapers were in a large, heavy binder. He flipped back to Saturday's paper and started on page 1. Concorde crashes in France. President holds Mideast peace talks. Update from an AIDS conference in Africa. He wondered if his mother would be upset that her disappearance wasn't front-page news in her own paper.

He almost missed it, there on page 16, a few paragraphs nestled alongside a big advertisement for Hubcap Heaven. A brief, his mother called these stories. He would have flipped right past it if not for the photograph. A tiny black-and-white mug shot of his mother. He had seen this picture of her in the newspaper before because occasionally she wrote a column—usually, embarrassingly, about something he or his brothers had done. It was an old photograph. She looked younger. And pretty. Patrick never thought about his mother being pretty. It took less than two minutes to read the entire story:

Newsday Employee Reported Missing

FARMINGDALE—The Nassau County Sheriff's Department confirmed Friday that Bernadette McBride, a longtime *Newsday* reporter and the mother of three, has been missing since September 7.

McBride, 40, of Farmingdale, left home shortly after 7 p.m. September 7 in her 1994 Volvo station wagon, according to her husband, Gerard McBride, a Farmingdale obstetrician.

"She was headed to her mother's house to finish some writing," McBride said.

The family has not heard from her since. Investigators searched that home, located in North Massapequa, and found no signs of foul play. The car, which was parked in the driveway, did not appear to have been tampered with.

"Being a missing person is not a crime," said Sgt. Robert Murray. "However, it is unusual for someone like Mrs. McBride not to be heard from for this length of time. We are concerned, and her family, obviously, is concerned." Murray asks that anyone with information about McBride call the Crime Stoppers hotline, 1-800-577-TIPS.

Bernadette McBride is five-foot-two, approximately 120 pounds, with brown hair and green eyes.

Patrick read the item twice, each time thinking how horrified his mother would be to see her age and weight in the newspaper.

He turned to Saturday's classifieds and scanned those, too, then Sunday's—the classifieds and the personals. Maybe she would send them a message through the newspaper. She and Kevin loved to read the classifieds and the personals. They would laugh uproariously at the junk people were trying to sell, including themselves. He turned back to the brief and looked over his shoulder at Mrs. Fitzjames, who was still standing over a cardboard box, reading the flaps of new books as she removed the jackets. He quietly folded and creased the newsprint. He took one more look over his shoulder before gently tugging at the sheet. It ripped easily. He folded it in half and put it in his pants pocket. He ruffled the pages to a different day's news and shrugged his backpack onto his right shoulder. "Thank you," he called to Mrs. Fitzjames, his front foot out the door before she had a chance to reply.

Outside, the rain continued to fall. Patrick didn't go out of his way to avoid puddles. He splashed along the path back to the main building, dragging his feet through the gullies.

By the time he got to the gym, he was twenty minutes late. He slipped into the locker room, changed into his shorts, and carried his wet shoes and socks out to the gym in his hands. He had lucked out. The rain must have scuttled whatever plan the teacher had, because it looked like a free-choice day. Small groups of kids were clustered around different equipment in the gymnasium. Patrick joined a group of boys he knew climbing rope. The teacher, Mr. Lewis, was working with a group of girls at the opposite end of the gym. He had a metal rack of basketballs wheeled up to the free-throw line and was running a drill on foul shooting. Patrick waited five minutes before walking over.

"Mr. Lewis, I didn't hear you call my name during attendance. My shoes were wet from going to the media center last class, so I went back into the locker room to get a dry pair of socks. But I didn't have any anyway."

"What's your last name?" Mr. Lewis asked, picking up his clipboard from the rack, where it had been standing at attention, wedged between two basketballs.

"McBride."

"Good thing you checked. I had you marked absent."

Patrick padded back to the rope-climbing area. He didn't want to climb, so he hung behind the group, thinking about the newspaper article, which made his mother's disappearance seem real and sound almost sinister. He thought guiltily about how he and his mother hadn't been getting along. She always wanted to take him places he could easily get to on his bike. He had found himself wishing he was older, old enough to drive a car. To have his own phone. His own room. To have a job. He had found himself, sometimes, wishing she would go away.

I didn't mean it, he thought, wanting more than ever a sign that she was okay. A note in the classifieds. Smoke signals. A message on the answering machine. Then he got an idea.

Patrick remembered his mother had her laptop with her when she left. When the bell rang after math, he raced to eighth period, Computer Literacy.

On Friday, Ms. Dobbs had walked them through setting up e-mail accounts and Internet etiquette and rules, which, if broken, would get you kicked out of Computer Literacy. Today they could start swapping messages.

He got to the classroom before anybody else and quickly fired up his monitor. He moved the mouse to the icon for e-mail, then dragged it down to **Write Mail**.

He typed in:

To: bmcbride@newsday.com
From: pmcbride@saltzmanms.edu
Subject: Hello from your firstborn
Date: 9/14 2:24:48 PM Daylight Saving Time

Hi, Mom. Where are you?

BERNADETTE

SEPTEMBER 14–18

After the first week, Bernadette gave up hoping she would simply wake up one morning restored to her previous life. But she was no closer to understanding what had happened to her or how to undo it. She realized it would be up to her to figure out how to get back to her family. And until she did, she needed to know they were okay without her.

She kept an eye on Patrick in class, though he appeared to have taken no notice of her. And every day she took the long way home so she could pass the house. She had seen Neil and Kevin, too—playing basketball in the driveway or riding their bikes—and they, too, appeared to be surviving without her. One day she passed Gerard on the sidewalk, out with Bran for a walk. She saw him coming before he noticed her, and her heart thumped so loud she was sure he would hear it.

Briefly, she considered screaming, *"It's me!"* But she decided against it, worried that if he had a heart attack, she'd have made her children orphans.

She wondered if anyone in her family had thought it unusual to see her walk by each day, but what would they see? A short, ponytailed girl walking along the sidewalk on the other side of the street, squinting at their home every afternoon, carrying a load of books or a bag of groceries.

One afternoon, when she turned onto Jackson Avenue, she saw Neil on her side of the street, drawing on the sidewalk outside the Yablonskis'. She briefly considered crossing the street to avoid talking to him—only because she was afraid she might cry. She steeled herself and kept walking.

"Hi," he said as she strode by.

"Hi," Bernadette responded. She stopped. "Whatcha drawing?"

"The beach—see? This is the lighthouse," he said.

"Very pretty. Are you missing summer?" she said.

"No—this is where my mother is. She's on vacation," he told her.

"Oh." Her heart sank. That must have been what Gerard had told him—that she was on vacation. Well, she was, sort of. "You doing okay without her?" she asked, but immediately regretted it.

"Yeah—but you should see our house. It's a pigsty!"

Bernadette stifled a laugh. "Oh, I'm sure your mother doesn't care about that," she said, a wave of relief flooding her. Until she asked the question, she didn't realize how terrified she'd be of his answer.

Just then Bobby Yablonski came barreling down the driveway on a skateboard. "C'mon, Neil. Let's go," he said.

"See ya," Neil said, running after Bobby.

Where is he going? she wondered. He's not allowed to go off by himself with Bobby.

She hadn't moved and Neil seemed to read her thoughts. "Bobby's teaching me to skateboard," he said.

"You should get your bike helmet," she said.

"Oh, you're right," he said. "Be right back, Bobby."

Bernadette watched him cross the street. Then she forced herself to move on.

So the house is a pigsty, she thought. Too bad I don't have an excuse to ring the doorbell. I'd love to take a peek. What would she need to pretend to be selling candy? An order form of some kind. She resolved to find a group at school that *was* doing fund-raising.

From the outside, the house looked the same (what was she expecting?), though there was a poster tacked to the telephone pole in the right-of-way, the bottom flapping in the wind stirred up by passing cars. She couldn't read it from across the street, which got her thinking about how old she was when she got glasses. Eighth grade, she remembered.

Bernadette had tried several times to question her mother, gently, to see what she knew about what had happened. But without knowing why, Bernadette understood that her mother did not remember her youngest daughter had grown up, married, and had three children of her own.

"Mom," she had asked her one evening over the weekend, "do you know anything about time travel?"

"Time travel?"

"Or reincarnation?"

"Is this for school?"

"No . . . well, yes, sort of. I'm just wondering about whether, say, you die—do you go back to your old life?"

"No, I don't believe so," her mother said.

"Well, then, is it possible, during your lifetime, to revisit earlier parts of it, and how that would happen? And if it did happen, how would you get back to the future part of it?"

"Bernadette, you're not making any sense."

"I know." Bernadette was sure her mother had no idea what she was talking about, and she was afraid to press it because she didn't think she could bring herself to tell her mother she was dead.

Even when Bernadette asked about the cures for various ills she remembered taking in childhood, her mother seemed confused by her sudden interest.

"You're writing this down?" her mother asked, startled to see Bernadette scribbling on a pad.

"Just practicing my note taking," Bernadette told her, but after that, she put the pen down and picked up her book. "Some of those teachers talk really fast." She'd felt her mother's eyes on her, staring, as if she, too, were trying to puzzle out what was happening.

So it was a very quiet existence, just the two of them. Fiona had always been a homebody, but Bernadette noticed she never left the house now, except to work in the garden, which had sprung to life under her care, though Bernadette hadn't tended it through the spring and summer. The phone never rang. (Who would be calling?) There didn't even seem to be any mail.

Every morning, Fiona left a paper sack on the counter containing a bread-and-butter sandwich or sliced bananas and sugar, a cold potato cut open and salted, and an oatmeal cookie. Often, the sack would also contain a short list and a few dollars. The worst part of the day involved getting dressed, as Bernadette struggled to assemble from her wardrobe of thirty-year-old clothing the least outlandish combination possible.

But she had been accepted at school as twelve-year-old Detta Downey. Mrs. Piazza didn't look twice at the birth certificate before slotting it into a file. Bernadette had scrambled the last four digits of her own Social Security number and penciled it in on the forms. It wasn't as if anybody was going to check. She had forged her mother's signature on a bunch of forms, changing her mother's first name, too. She couldn't manufacture medical records, so one afternoon she had gone to the health department, a two-story brick building on Main Street, rolled up her sleeve for a nurse, and looked the other way. It hurt a lot less than labor pains.

Surprisingly, she was enjoying seventh grade. School was not the miserable prison existence she remembered. Her favorite class was social studies, because the teacher, Mr. Posnak, was educated and funny. "I'm simplifying this, but I'll try to make it as boring as it would be in detail," he said during one lecture, which covered an entire century of European history. Bernadette laughed out loud and drew looks.

Mr. Posnak was a slight, middle-aged man, reed-thin and practically bald, but he had a lot of authority, which allowed him to actually teach. The antics of a few boys, rocking back and forth in their chairs, vrooming their desks from side to side, suspending pencils from nostrils, clearly unnerved some teachers to the point that little teaching got done. Mr. Grizzard, who taught chemistry, spent more time rearranging students to separate troublemakers than he did on his lesson plan. In chemistry, however, this was important, as the combination of boys and certain reagents was highly combustible.

The Baxter twins sat behind her in that class. Just the day before, she had been copying notes Mr. Grizzard put on the board when a loud *crack* split the air. Bernadette twisted backward to see where the sound had come from. Her lab partner dove under the desk.

Kyle and Duffy were frosted with white foam, laughing.

"That was awesome!" one of the twins said. (Bernadette never could tell them apart.)

After that, Mr. Grizzard put the baking soda and vinegar under lock and key and put the Baxter boys at separate tables on opposite ends of the front row.

Mr. Posnak mostly ignored the nonsense, although occasionally he would call out a name and that person would come and sit on the floor in the front of the room with his—always *his*—back to the class for the rest of the period. Mr. Posnak would make no other comment about the behavior. Just the name and a gesture at the spot on the linoleum where the offender should park. Bernadette was awed by the nerve it took to do this when some of these boys were big enough to take out Mr. Posnak with one swipe of a paw.

The class was starting a unit on immigration, which Bernadette had always wanted to learn more about. She never had time to do more than occasionally catch part of a program on PBS. For her paper, she planned to go to the public library and get several books she had been meaning to read for years. *Angela's Ashes* and *How the Irish Saved Civilization* had been sitting on her bedside table, unread, since several Christmases ago. Too bad she couldn't run in and get them now. Bernadette had forgotten how many empty hours there were after school and homework and before sleep. She had read more books in three weeks than she had in the past three years and was running out of material at her mother's house. She could walk to the public library, but she had a hazy recollection that she wouldn't be allowed to get a library card, at her age, without a parent. *Bernadette* had a library card, of course, but she worried that somebody would recognize the name if Detta Downey tried to use it. Bernadette knew that in her other life she was a familiar face in the library—getting books for Patrick and Kevin, bringing Neil to story hour.

Mr. Posnak drew a chalk line on the blackboard the length of the room and hash marks every few feet. The moment the bell rang, as was his custom, he shut the door and began talking.

"We have folkloric images of immigrants, ideas which suit our vision of ourselves as a great nation," he said, slip-slapping his hands together to shake the chalk dust from them. "Those who immigrated to our shores were the 'cream of the crop' in their own countries, full of the entrepreneurial spirit, headed to the 'land of opportunity' to seek their fortunes. Stop me if you've heard this before." A few people laughed.

Bernadette could see where he was going. Her mother hadn't left Ireland; she was pushed. By custom, only boys inherited land in Ireland, unless a family was unlucky enough to have produced no sons. Fiona had two brothers and five sisters. There was no money to send daughters to school beyond eighth grade and no jobs for women without an education. One of Bernadette's uncles had become a priest. The other ran the farm. One aunt was a nun. Everyone else had come to America.

"Okay, forget all that," Mr. Posnak continued. "It isn't true. Few immigrants came to America ready to start their own dot-coms—or whatever the equivalent was when they arrived. Can anybody tell me what the best example of this is?"

Nobody raised a hand. Nobody ever raised a hand, Bernadette noticed. She didn't either.

Mr. Posnak wrote *1492* on the first hash mark and drew an arrow to the second mark, which he labeled *1812*.

"The largest group of immigrants to America in the first three hundred years of its settlement by Europeans came from Africa, and not a one of them came here with intentions of making a fortune." Mr. Posnak started writing place-names on the board: *Charleston, New Orleans, Savannah*.

Mr. Posnak continued, talking about the steps taken to "assimilate" Africans—taking away their names and their language, prohibiting them from marrying, breaking up families on the auction block. Bernadette thought about her parents, who had been in their early twenties when they arrived in New York in the 1950s. Her mother hadn't wanted to leave home either, but at least she hadn't been dragged away in chains. Once here, Fiona simply refused to assimilate—an option not available to Africans, Bernadette thought. Her father, on the other hand, had become thoroughly Americanized. He joined the army because, after serving, the government would pay his way through college.

He followed New York's sports teams. He learned to drive and pleaded with Fiona to do the same so he wouldn't have to ferry her everywhere.

When Bernadette came out of her daydream, she had missed a hundred years of history. Mr. Posnak was in his customary gallop through time. The newest hash mark on the board read *1902* and he was talking about Teddy Roosevelt's fears that America could not continue to absorb a million immigrants a year. The girl to Bernadette's left was furiously taking notes. Bernadette copied Mr. Posnak's time line from the board. It *did* look like quiz material.

By the end of the class, Mr. Posnak was talking about Haitian refugees and Cuban rafters, the porous Tex-Mex border and the fall of Communism in Eastern Europe. The whole board was filled with place-names and numbers. He put the chalk in the tray and brushed his hands together again.

"Okay, the point of this survey," he said, gesturing at the blackboard, "is to get you thinking about where we all come from." He picked up a stack of photocopies from his desk. "The paper for this unit is an essay on your family's personal immigration story."

He counted the number of students in each row and handed several sheets to the first student in each row.

"Pass these back please. You can use the library, oral history, the Web, but—as I've outlined here on this handy instruction sheet—you must place your family's history in the context of the larger immigration of their people to the U.S. This will mean you can't just interview Grandpa and write down what he says. The only person exempted from this is, of course, Ms. Downey, whose immigration experience can be a first-person account."

Detta looked up from her notebook, feeling her cheeks redden. Mr. Posnak wore a slight smile and appeared to be waiting for her to respond.

"Well, I was born here. Technically, I'm not an immigrant," she managed.

"Ah! Out-migration and in-migration. You have a *lot* of explaining to do," he said.

If only you knew, Bernadette thought, if only you knew.

Patrick

To: bmcbride@newsday.com
From: pmcbride@saltzmanms.edu
Subject: Help
Date: 09/16 2:36:12 PM Daylight Saving Time

Hi, Mom. I know you haven't answered my last e-mail. I guess you haven't been able to sign on in a while. Whenever you can write back is okay. I just thought I'd let you know that we are missing you at home.

The house is a mess. Not that I'm trying to upset you. It's just that, if you are headed home, you could send me an e-mail and we'll clean up before you get there. I've been taking the garbage out, but nobody puts recyclables in the bin. Dad throws the newspapers in with the regular garbage, although I asked him nicely not to.

Kevin won't put his dirty clothes in the hamper. They're thrown all over the room. Not that I'm being a tattletale. The point is that nobody listens to me. Dad tries to do laundry when he gets home, but he starts a load and then forgets to put the clean clothes in the dryer. By the time he does remember, the wet clothes have gotten moldy and no amount of Snuggles or Softie will make them smell like Mountain Breezes or Springtime or whatever it is they're supposed to smell like. They smell like the basement. Neil has gone to school smelling like that a few days because at least the clothes were technically clean. You had to get really close to him to notice the odor.

That's not the worst of it with Neil, though. He has like a ring of peanut butter and tomato sauce around his mouth. He won't hold still long enough for me to wipe it off. It's like crusted on there. Even after a bath, it still looks like his face is dirty. Kevin is no help. He just laughs.

We have eaten a lot of pizza. I think even Kevin now would go for something homemade. I made scrambled eggs one night, and believe it or not, he ate that! With toast. I think it was like the healthiest thing Kevin has ever eaten. Neil has eaten a lot of Happy Meals because, well, it makes him happy, and Dad is into making him happy.

Also, do we have a mop? The kitchen floor has something sticky on it. I tried to sweep up, but that didn't do it.

It almost doesn't matter, because there's not much to eat in the kitchen anymore. We've been eating out a LOT. Since we ran out of pizza, anyway. We're out of Pop-Tarts, Cinnamon Toast Crunch, Fudge sandwich cookies, Rice Krispies bars, Cheese Nips, raisin boxes (which I had been putting in Neil's lunch, because we're out of grapes), fruit chews, juice boxes, and a lot of other stuff. For breakfast, I gave Neil All-Bran because it was the only cereal we had left except oatmeal, but he wouldn't eat that either. It did look disgusting. Dad told me to start a grocery list, which I did, but now I can't find it. Maybe I'll print out this e-mail when Ms. Dobbs isn't looking.

Every day Kevin says he has no homework, but I know he's lying. I've been in fifth grade and there's homework every day, except like the day before Christmas vacation. He totally ignores me, though, and Dad says it is the least of his worries. I'd hate to see Kevin's report card, though. I told him he would be in big trouble, but he could care less what I tell him.

School for me is okay. This class is pretty good. I like to send e-mail. It's like having a diary only not as dorky. Only girls have diaries, right, Mom? :) I like social studies, too. The teacher is Mr. Posnak. He is a good teacher, but he gives a lot of work. We have to write a paper on our family's "immigration history." That made me miss Grandma because I know she would give me an earful. Instead I went to the library, and Mrs. Fitzjames, you know the lady from church? She's our librarian. She showed me some books and I read one, about the Irish Brigade. They fought in the U.S. Civil War. Anyway, it was a good book, but I guess I can't see how it's going to help me with my own family's immigration history. I don't think any of our relatives were around here when the Civil War was going on. So if you could get back before the paper is due, that would help, because I have a lot of questions Dad doesn't have the answers for. If you don't get back soon, I will have to do Dad's side of the family, which is not as easy, since, according to him, he is a "mutt" and his relatives are from all over Europe, not one place. Since I already started the research on Ireland, it would be better if I could stick with that, right? If you can't get back, could you send me an e-mail with some information?

Neil misses you. And Dad, too, but he has a hard time talking about it. Kevin's personal relationship with the remote control has gotten even deeper. If the remote control was missing, THAT would get his attention.

Please come home. Please write back. We'll be good.

To: bmcbride@newsday.com
From: pmcbride@saltzmanms.edu
Subject: My last message
Date: 09/17 2:24:48 PM Daylight Saving Time

Mom, I reread the last e-mail I sent you, because I did print it out so I could recopy the stuff we need from the grocery store, and I realized it might make you more reluctant to come home because things sound bad. But I have good news! Dad hired a cleaning lady. She started yesterday and she worked all day. There were tall piles of clean clothes on my dresser and Kevin's dresser to put away when I got home from school. Kevin's had fallen over by the time we went to bed, but, hey!, at least the clothes on the floor now are clean clothes!

Dad also told us last night that he is going to get somebody to come over in the afternoons to help us with our homework—he looked directly at Kevin as he was saying this, but would Kevin know? No, because Kevin was playing his Game Boy while Dad was talking and might as well have been on Planet Xenon for all he heard of what Dad said.

Also, I should have told you that we all miss you a lot, but we have been getting along okay. Dad is home earlier from work than normal and he's taken us to miniature golf and the movies. That's been fun.

To: bmcbride@newsday.com
From: pmcbride@saltzmanms.edu
Subject: Neil's essay
Date: 09/21 2:48:12 PM Daylight Saving Time

Mom, I know you would have loved this. Dad laughed, and that was the first time I heard him laugh in a while. Neil had to write an essay for school. Dad said, "That is absurd! He can barely write at all!" Neil got all insulted and said, "I can too write and Mrs. Green says don't worry about spelling yet. Write down your ideas and we'll work on the spelling later." And then I told Dad, it's not that crazy because I think next year in third grade is when they make everybody take those timed essay tests, so the teachers start practicing as soon as you can write about four words in a row. Then Kevin, who has lost his TV privileges for a week because his math teacher called Dad and said he hadn't turned in a single homework sheet yet, jumped right in. Scholar that he is, he said he knew exactly how to write an essay. Well, both Dad and I pushed back our chairs, thinking, This we got to see.

So Kevin asks Neil, "What's the topic?"

"It can be on any topic," Neil said, "but it has to be four sentences."

"Great. All you do, Neil, is, say the essay is about"—and here Kevin looked around for something to write about—"say the essay is about Rugrats Fruit Snacks," and he put the box on the table in front of Neil. (Oh, Dad got to the grocery store, finally.) "Your first sentence is 'Rugrats Fruit Snacks'—you can copy the words right off the box—'are . . .' and now come up with what they are."

"What are they?"

"I don't know. You're the one that eats them. You have to describe what they are."

"Made with real fruit? That's right on the box, too."

"Perfect. Now write that down."

Neil scribbled away and then Kevin says, "Now the second sentence, you change the words in the first sentence around. Like, 'There is real fruit in Rugrats Fruit Snacks.'" Neil wrote that down, too.

"You're on second base, buddy. Now, the third sentence is the trickiest because they always want you to add a new fact. What else do you know about Rugrats Fruit Snacks?"

"I don't know."

"Neil, boy, I can't do *all* your work for you. Think of something."

"They're different colors?"

"Fabulous. Now make it into a sentence, like 'Rugrats Fruit Snacks are different colors.' You're ninety feet from home plate. You only need a conclusion, which is the first sentence said in a different way."

"What kind of different way?"

"Mix up the words again."

"Like 'Real fruit is a part of Rugrats Fruit Snacks'?"

"Neil, you are a natural. Write that down, buddy. You're home free."

Well, by this time Dad could not stop laughing. He asked Kevin who taught him this fascinating method of essay writing and Kevin said Mrs. Rodgers, his third-grade teacher. Dad kind of grunted, but he let it go.

Then, yesterday, Neil came home and the teacher had written *Excellent*! with a smiley face on the top of his essay.

And today Dad said his No. 1 priority was finding us a tutor.

To: bmcbride@newsday.com
From: pmcbride@saltzmanms.edu
Subject: The accident
Date: 09/22 3:00:24 PM Daylight Saving Time

Mom, not to worry you or anything, but when you come home, Kevin will look weirder. He's okay, though. Well, as okay as he ever was.

What happened was Kevin was in the backyard trying to teach Neil the perkle slide. (That's when you jump up and down on your skateboard on top of a picnic table.) When he landed, his board wheeled right out from under him and he lost his balance and came down on his elbow and the side of his head. I only heard the thud and then him wailing, "My arm!" Of course he wasn't wearing pads or a lid. His head is okay, but he got a big gash on his scalp and had to get twenty-four stitches and he has a big bald spot where they shaved off his hair. His arm is in a cast, a soft cast, but it's not broken, just dislocated. He kinda twisted it backward. When I went racing out there, it was sticking out at a weird angle, like you could do with Gumby's arm? It hurt just to look at it.

Dad was on it, though. I never saw him move so fast. He made me get ice and towels and his emergency kit, and then he took Kevin to the hospital for an X ray. Neil cried, but not until after Dad and Kevin left. I think he was scared for Kevin, and he told me he doesn't want to learn to skateboard anymore.

Kevin, I have to say, didn't cry. I think he was stunned. Then, when he got home, he was back to his old self. He said he'd have to become a switch-hitter and learn to use the remote with his left hand. So, everything's back to normal. Dad says maybe he will have to hire a full-time nurse, too.

To: bmcbride@newsday.com
From: pmcbride@saltzmanms.edu
Subject: The new tutor
Date: 09/23 2:36:00 PM Daylight Saving Time

The new tutor is a college student named Brent. He came over yesterday to meet us. He looks young, I guess because he is short, but he's smart, Dad says, and he knows first aid because he works as a camp counselor during the summer. He's going to be here Tuesdays and Thursdays. Kevin is bumming because that will cut into his TV-watching ways. He stayed home from school yesterday because he was achy from falling. Today, Dad made him go. He's got a big bandage plastered to the side of his head. He put on a ski cap to cover it. Dad told him to be careful not to go near the 7-Eleven, because he looks like he might be planning to rob it.

To: bmcbride@newsday.com
From: pmcbride@saltzmanms.edu
Subject: Kevin's dome
Date: 09/24 2:36:12 PM Daylight Saving Time

Well, Kevin was not allowed to wear the ski cap at school and his friends razzed him for laying a flip and having half his hair missing. So yesterday Dad took him to the barber and he got the rest of it shaved off. He finally looks like the true freak he really is.

To: bmcbride@newsday.com
From: pmcbride@saltzmanms.edu
Subject: No subject
Date: 09/25 2:48:36 PM Daylight Saving Time

Hi, Mom. We had a surprise quiz in this class today. Think I did okay, though.

Dad had big news yesterday—he delivered triplets. It wasn't his patient, but he was on call last night. The babies were early, I think. He said you would have been happy for the mom. She didn't want to know whether the babies were boys or girls before they were born. Dad said the sex of the babies wasn't marked on her chart and that's unusual these days, so there was a lot of excitement in the delivery room. The first baby came out and it was a boy. The second baby came out and it was a boy. And then the nurses started whooping and hollering when the last baby came out because it was a girl. Dad said a tear actually came to his eye and that was the first time that had happened in a long time, since he's gotten so used to everything that can happen in a delivery room. And then he said, "I wish your mother could've been there. She would have cried, too. Of happiness." I thought I would tell you that story. It made me think you wish you had a daughter.

I'm not really expecting to get answers to these e-mails, but it makes me feel better to write them. Where is your laptop? I know you took it with you. Where are you?

BERNADETTE

Bernadette was scribbling furiously in her notebook. Mr. Posnak had started a unit on women in American history. But when he made a joke about Hillary Clinton channeling Eleanor Roosevelt for inspiration and advice, everyone laughed but Bernadette.

The word "channeling" had stopped her pen. A month ago she would have laughed, too, because she was highly skeptical of supposedly paranormal phenomena. But something supernatural had certainly happened to her.

She looked out the classroom windows at the red-and-gold maple leaves twirling to the ground. What if, she thought, what happened to me had happened to someone else? What if it was a news tip I was assigned to check out? Sure, plenty of tips don't check out and plenty of wackos call the paper, but what if a seemingly sane and persuasive twelve-year-old told her, *I used to be forty.* What if this girl said she had three kids, and, indeed, there were three kids whose mother had disappeared? What if the girl's story checked out? How would I go about investigating that? Surely, I wouldn't just dismiss it, would I?

No, I would research it, Bernadette thought. I would call experts. I would start reading, to find out if there were any similar occurrences on record.

WHY HAVEN'T I DONE ANY OF THAT??? she wondered, unconsciously banging her fist in anger—at herself—on her desk.

"Miss Downey?" Mr. Posnak asked.

"Sorry." She thought he looked startled. She prayed he wasn't going to make her sit on the floor in the corner with her back to the class. But he just stared at her an extra second and then went back to his lecture.

Bernadette started writing again—trying to word-associate with all the topics she had once dismissed as nonsense: reincarnation, out-of-body experiences, near-death experiences, soul switching. What else? ESP, past lives, the afterlife, spirit guides. Was there more? Think, think, Bernadette.

Then the bell rang, and Bernadette promised herself a trip to the library right after school.

After history, Bernadette waited at her locker, as she did every day, for Donna and her friends—Judy and Annmarie— who had made a place for her at lunch. Though Bernadette was wary of actually making a friend, unsure of how she'd answer questions a real friend would have, she understood the importance of traveling in a pack in middle school. It was a survival thing.

Bernadette and Annmarie both brought lunch from home, so they got a table each day. Annmarie had taken it upon herself to try to explain who was who among the seventh-grade social cliques.

"See that girl? In the fleece vest? That's Mina. Her best friend is Erica, the one in the long-sleeve Gap T-shirt. But Caitlyn—see that girl in the flower-print scoop neck?—she thinks Erica is *her* best friend, but she hates Mina."

"How does Erica explain why she sits with Mina at lunch?" Bernadette asked.

"Oh. See that girl in the pashmina sweater set sitting with Caitlyn? That's Katie. Erica and Katie hate each other because they both went steady with Kyle Baxter, so Erica told Caitlyn—"

"Kyle Baxter went steady with someone?" Bernadette felt dizzy trying to keep up with Annmarie's commentary.

"Someone? He's a *serial* dumper."

"Serial dumper?"

"He collects girlfriends like you and I collect gel pens."

Donna and Judy arrived with their trays, and Bernadette was rescued from having to come up with a way of asking whether Patrick McBride was a serial dumper. She honestly didn't think she wanted to know. She had forgotten how confusing it was to be not quite a kid and not yet an adult.

"The Backstreet Boys are playing at the Nassau Coliseum in November!" Judy announced, setting her plastic tray on the lunch table.

"Are you going to go?" Annmarie asked.

"We should all go," Donna said.

"I could ask my father if he'd drive us. How much are the tickets?" Annmarie said.

"Expensive, but I have money from baby-sitting," Judy

said. "What about you, Detta? Don't you love the Backstreet Boys?"

"Oh . . ." Bernadette had a vague idea Patrick didn't like the Backstreet Boys. "Lame" was the word she remembered him using.

"Detta might not know who the Backstreet Boys are," Donna interjected. "Do they play the same music in Ireland?"

Did they? Bernadette had no idea. "Well, they have radio," she stammered, trying to think of an answer that wouldn't trip her up later. Just then a voice at her left asked, "Anybody sitting here?"

She put her sandwich down to move her book bag off the seat beside her. As she turned to reach it, a black suede boot kicked the bag to the floor.

"Oops." It was Victoria, the blond from computer class, holding a tray with a large drink on it. Across the table, Bernadette saw Victoria's sidekick, the one who had wanted the seat Bernadette grabbed, drop her chin to her chest and laugh.

Victoria let the tray slip out of her hands and stepped back. It made a clanging sound on the table. The soda wobbled and toppled with an icy splash. A lake of liquid spread quickly, cascading over the side and onto Bernadette's lap. She stood up in a rush and watched Donna do the same, trying to move away from the spilling soda, but both of them had rust-colored splotches on their shirtfronts.

"Oops, again!" Victoria said. She had moved away the moment she dropped the tray. "Oh well, I wasn't thirsty anyway. C'mon, Kristen, let's go." The two linked arms and sauntered off.

"That . . . girl!" Bernadette was fuming. "She is lucky I'm not her mother." Then she realized what she said. Donna and Annmarie were giving her a funny look. "I mean, she is lucky I don't *tell* her mother." Change the subject, quick, Bernadette thought. "Donna—did you get all wet?"

"A little," she said.

Judy had run up to the lunch line and come back with a stack of napkins and a rag.

"What was *that* about?" she asked, looking directly at Bernadette. Donna and Bernadette split the stack of napkins in two and started mopping.

"She can't get over the fact that I took the seat next to her in computer class and she was saving it for her friend. She's been harassing me for weeks."

All three girls nodded in understanding. Donna was trying to blot the stains on her blouse. "She's a jerk, Detta. Is that the only class you have with her?"

"No, she's in my gym class, too. Both of them are. Oh, I just thought of something."

"What?"

"One day last week, after gym, when I went to change back into my clothes, they were all wet."

"Sopping wet?" Annmarie asked.

"Yes," Bernadette replied.

"The clothes shower." Annmarie said.

"What's that?" Bernadette asked.

"My sister told me there was a girl in her class, who nobody liked? They put all her clothes in the shower stall and turned the water on. Then, after they were soaked, they hung them back in the girl's locker."

"You're kidding!" Bernadette said. Were kids this nasty

when she was in seventh grade? Yes, she remembered, they were. A few of them.

"My sister said everybody knew who did it, but nobody said anything because they didn't want it done to their clothes next."

Bernadette was sure Victoria had pulled the same stunt. She hadn't made the connection then, but now she remembered that in computer class that day Victoria had repeatedly asked her friend, "Does it smell moldy to you in here? I distinctly smell mold." At the time Bernadette had thought she was making a weak joke about body odor.

"Did you put your wet clothes back on?" Judy asked.

"Well, no. I tried to dry my shirt under the hand dryer, but it would've taken hours, so I wore my gym clothes for the rest of the day. I had a jacket in my other locker. I wore it over them."

"I remember that," Donna said. "I thought it was weird, but . . . I didn't think to ask."

Bernadette knew Donna was too polite to say that her wardrobe was *always* weird.

"It never occurred to me that somebody would do that on purpose," Bernadette said, sponging wet spots on her shirt with a dry napkin. "I was looking at the top of the locker to see if there was a leak in the ceiling or a burst pipe."

"Don't you have a lock for gym?" Donna asked.

"No."

"You better get one," Annmarie said.

After lunch, Donna and Bernadette walked to math class.

"I'm sorry about your shirt," Bernadette told her.

"It's just a shirt," Donna said. "Lucky you're wearing those brown polka dots. The stains blend in." They were standing at Donna's locker while Donna swapped books from her backpack with the ones she'd need for her afternoon classes.

I am lucky, Bernadette thought. Lucky Mrs. Piazza had introduced her to Donna and not someone like Victoria. Then she realized luck had nothing to do with it. Mrs. Piazza knew better.

"Detta, do you have any friends in that gym class?" Donna asked as they settled into their seats in math.

"I don't have any friends except you and Judy and Annmarie."

"That is pathetic, Detta. What period is it?"

"Fifth."

"No, gym class. What period is your gym class?"

"Oh—second."

"I'll meet you outside the gym tomorrow before class. Don't go into the locker room. Get there as early as you can."

While Mrs. Fermat was droning on about the value of X and Y, Bernadette was trying to calculate how much cash she had left. She would need to go to the hardware store to get a lock. There was a lock on her mother's garden shed, but though she had scoured the house, she couldn't find the key for it. With all her grocery-store purchases, she knew she had no more than one twenty-dollar bill left.

She went directly home after school and got her overnight bag out from behind the vent. She had twenty-four dollars and a lot of change. She took her ATM card and her library card from their leather slots and tucked them into the pocket of her hip-hugger jeans.

Her mother must have been in the backyard, because the house was empty. She peered out the kitchen window, expecting to see her gardening, but she wasn't there. There was a small black rabbit gnawing on a green bean. How funny, she thought. She had often seen a black rabbit in the yard when she was growing up, but she hadn't seen one in years. There must be a family of them living in the woods. Her mother wouldn't like to see this one eating her crop, though. Bernadette wondered where she was—down in the basement?—but left without finding her, since she had a lot to do.

She went to the ATM outside the grocery store first, withdrawing three hundred dollars, the most it would give her. The money came out in a stack of twenty-dollar bills. Bernadette had to inhale to squeeze the thick wedge of folded money into her front pocket.

"Why, hello, Detta Downey," came a voice from a woman pushing a cart out the automatic door. It was Mrs. Piazza.

Bernadette was too stunned to react, but Mrs. Piazza hadn't even slowed down. "Hello," she murmured, waving at Mrs. Piazza's back. Had she seen her at the machine?

Bernadette quickly stepped on the rubber mat to activate the door and walked into the cool air of the supermarket. Why was her heart racing? She walked through a few aisles to calm down before heading to the hardware store. She bought the cheapest lock they had, knowing this cash would have to last until she found a way home. *Please* let me find a way home, she thought. It was nerve-racking to worry about being caught in all the lies she'd told.

At the library, she stopped first at the checkout desk. She didn't recognize the clerk. This was a good thing.

"Excuse me. How many books can you take out on one card?" Bernadette asked.

"Is it your card?"

What should she say?

"The reason I ask is that adults can take out a maximum of fifty items," the clerk said. "But if it's a child's card, you can only get ten."

"It's my mother's," she said, heading to the computer with the long list of topics she had written in the margin of her history notes.

Time to get busy.

PATRICK

THURSDAY, OCTOBER 1

Each day Patrick went to school hopeful it would be the day his mother answered his e-mails. Each day he was disappointed. Disappointment grew to frustration. No one was doing anything to find his mother. He had asked his father again about calling the police in Nashville, but he shook his head no.

"Patrick, that was just something your mother said as a joke. She knows she can't sing."

"I don't think so, Dad," Patrick insisted. Maybe his father didn't realize how many times she had said it.

So Patrick gave up waiting for someone *else* to do something.

He went to the library on his way home because he knew, from having watched his mother use it, that the reference desk had a CD-ROM with phone numbers for the entire country. He needed a few out-of-state telephone numbers. If he got them from the library, without a 411 charge showing up on the telephone bill, maybe his father wouldn't no- tice a few long-distance calls. He quickly found what he needed and wrote the numbers in the margins of a math test he had gotten back.

As he was leaving, he saw the new girl who sat behind him in Computer Literacy at the desk, waiting to check out a huge stack of books. Wow, he thought, she must be a big reader. Patrick didn't know her name, but she seemed very nice. She always smiled at him. If he hadn't been in such a hurry, he would have asked if she needed help carrying the books home, but she had so many she must have been there with her mother or father—somebody with a car.

When he got home, Brent, the tutor, was in the kitchen with Neil. Kevin was slumped on the couch, watching *Jenny Jones.*

"What is this fascinating program about?" Patrick asked.

"Stripper makeovers."

"Very wholesome. No homework, again?"

"I did it already, *Mom,*" Kevin said.

"Shut up."

Patrick ducked his head into the kitchen, where Brent was sitting at the table with Neil, who was reading aloud an *Amelia Bedelia* book. There was an exotic smell, something spicy, coming from a pot on the stove. Brent was not only smart, he could cook. He was now making dinners for them on the afternoons he was there to help with homework. Patrick was thankful, because the novelty of cooking for his brothers had worn off, especially since half the time they wouldn't eat what he made.

"What's in the pot?" Patrick asked.

"Hello, Patrick, you're late, aren't you? It's chicken curry. One of my specialties."

"Smells good," Patrick said, but he was thinking, Good luck getting Kevin and Neil to eat that. "I'm going upstairs to do my homework."

"When I'm done with Neil, let's sit down for five minutes and go over what you've got coming up. Don't you have a report due soon in social studies?"

"It's written." Which was true.

"When do you have to turn it in?"

"October second."

Brent laughed. "You mean tomorrow. Where is it?"

"On the computer."

"File name?"

"IMMIGRATION. Can I go now?"

"Be gone," Brent said, turning back to Neil. He was nice, but Patrick had learned he was every bit as pesky about homework as his own mother. Patrick had gotten into a habit of telling his mother as little as possible about school because she would latch onto things. He remembered the time in fourth grade when he told her he had to write an essay on "Why education is important to me." She had wanted him to read a whole biography of Horace Mann, who had invented school or something like that.

"Mom, this essay only has to be one page," he remembered telling her.

"It can be a well-researched one page," she said. Sometimes she felt like a burr on his shoelace. Impossible to get rid of without feeling pain. He felt guilty now that he had thought that.

He went into his room and pulled a brown paper bag out from under his bed. Quietly, he crossed the hall to his mother's office, which was actually the extra bedroom—closed the door, and turned the button on the knob to lock it.

He took the telephone off his mother's desk and sat down with it on the carpet. He pulled the math test out of his pocket and dialed the first number.

"*The Tennessean.* How may I direct your call?" a woman said, in a singsong voice.

"Newsroom, please." Patrick waited while she transferred the call.

"City desk." Another woman's voice, although this one sounded younger.

"Yes, hello. I'm calling from New York about a missing person."

"I'm listening."

"Yes, her name is Bernadette McBride, she's five-foot-two, a hundred and twenty pounds—"

"I'm sorry," the woman cut in. "Why are you calling *The Tennessean?*"

"Isn't this the newspaper in Nashville?"

"Yes."

"Well, she may have been heading that way." Patrick had been trying to disguise his voice to sound older, but he sensed it wasn't working.

"Well, have you filed a missing-person report with the police?"

"What I was wondering is if there have been any stories about unknown women showing up there, maybe with amnesia?" Patrick said.

"Hang on."

Patrick listened to an advertisement about classified advertising and then another about *The Tennessean*'s award-winning sports section before a man's voice came on the line.

"Hello, this is Charles Clark. I'm one of the editors here. Who am I speaking to?"

"This is Patrick McBride."

"Patrick, the lady you were talking to filled me in. What was the woman's name you're looking for again?"

"Bernadette McBride."

"And how old is she?"

"Um, she's forty. She just turned forty." Why are newspapers so interested in a person's age? he wondered.

"Is she your mama?"

"Yes."

"And she's here, in Tennessee?"

"Well, I don't know. I mean, she's missing. And she always told us she was going to go to Nashville because she likes country music."

"I see. Well, Patrick, if the police here are looking for her, they haven't asked for our help. And we don't have any amnesia victims in the hospital right now, so I don't believe I can help you. Is your daddy there?"

"No, he's at work."

"Does he know you're calling us?"

"No."

"Well, I'll tell you what. This phone call will be between us men, okay? Give me your number. If your mama turns up here, I promise to call you."

"Thanks," Patrick said. He gave the number and hung up.

Rats, he thought. He had also gotten an 800 number for Greyhound bus lines. He figured if his mother had gone to Nashville without her car, she might have taken a cab to the bus station on Route 110 because she didn't like to fly. But he had lost enthusiasm. They probably didn't keep a record of who traveled where anyway.

He opened the brown bag and pulled out the road atlas, which he had sneaked out of his father's car. Patrick measured the mileage key with his pinkie. One pinkie length equaled three hundred miles. He laid his little finger across Tennessee and Virginia, marked his place, and measured again, across Maryland and New Jersey to Long Island. More than six hundred miles. What a joke, he thought. He could never get all the way to Tennessee by himself. Why couldn't his mother run away to the city, to the Metropolitan Museum of Art, like other people do?

He tried to think where else she might be. He closed his eyes to think about the last time he'd seen her. He'd had his headphones on, listening to a Red Hot Chili Peppers CD, when she pushed his bedroom door open. He had been expecting the nightly lecture about his daily misdeeds: Could he please not fight with Kevin? Could he please do his chores before the amp went on? Could he take fifteen minutes to play Candy Land with Neil?

"He worships you, Patrick," she'd tell him. He'd heard this speech a million times, so he didn't bother taking the headphones off. He knew what she was going to say.

He tried to remember when this had become their routine. When Patrick was little, bedtime had been his favorite time of day. He and Kevin would spread a blanket out on the floor and turn off all but the light in the closet. His mother would read them stories by flashlight. She was good at reading stories. She would put on accents and do different voices for each character. She could make a person cry about Horton the Elephant. In fact, she used to tear up herself occasionally over Horton almost losing that egg he had sat on so long and so well.

They had called this "the campfire," and every night after they brushed their teeth, Kevin and he would beg, Mom, can we please have a campfire? He could not remember his mother ever saying no.

Now, when he thought about it, he realized it had been years since they did that, and he couldn't remember why or when it stopped. Was it when Neil was born? Not that he would want to have a campfire now, but when did that end?

One wall of his mother's office was covered with framed photographs, mostly school pictures of Kevin and him, but along the top row were pictures of his father and mother when they were children. His father had hardly changed at all, but his mother's face had filled out and she had cut her hair short. Patrick looked at the girl in the photograph and wondered how old his mother was when it was taken. About the same age he was now. The girl in the photograph looked familiar, but she didn't really look like his mother. Even here in his mother's office, surrounded by all her things, Patrick was having trouble summoning up exactly what she looked like.

On the other hand, he had no problem hearing her voice. He'd put the dishes from dinner in the sink instead of the dishwasher or forget to put the shower curtain inside the tub, and he could hear what she'd say. Neil left his crayons on the table and Patrick heard himself telling Neil to put them away—like she would. The words had come easily, and Patrick realized how many times his mother had said the same exact thing, like a refrain.

But on the night she left, there was no lecture, no clue Patrick could follow now. Patrick remembered her looking at him so long it made him uncomfortable, so he looked away. And by the time he looked back, there was just an empty space where she had been.

BERNADETTE

FRİDAY, OCTOBER 2

The day after the cafeteria incident with Victoria, Bernadette sprinted from her first-period class to meet Donna outside the gym.

"Is Victoria here already?" Bernadette asked.

Donna shook her head. "I didn't look in the locker room, but I doubt she'd be early for gym," she said, craning her neck down the hallway to scan the crowd of students. Her eyes lit up and she called out, "Allison! Do you have gym now?"

"Hi, Donna, yeah. Why?"

"Ally, this is Detta Downey, she's new here. Can you watch out for her in this class? Her clothes got a shower last week."

"Those were yours? I saw that, but I didn't know who . . . gosh, I'm sorry. I should have said something, but nobody wants to mess with Victoria Cavendish. She is *so* evil."

Donna hushed them. "Shhh, here she comes with her satellite."

"Satellite?" Bernadette asked.

"Kristen Douglas," Donna whispered. "She's in orbit around the fabulous Victoria Cavendish."

"And she has about as much personality as a satellite, too," Ally said.

Bernadette wondered if Victoria and Kristen had all their classes together. How had they arranged that?

Donna heaved her book bag over her right shoulder and walked backward away from the gym, giving Bernadette a thumbs-up sign Victoria couldn't see. "Good luck," she mouthed silently.

"She is so nice," Bernadette said to Ally.

"She is nice. She won the Good Citizen Award at our elementary school. My mother says we'll be voting for her someday. For president."

"She's got my vote," Bernadette said, holding the locker-room door open for Ally.

On fair-weather days, like this one, the gym teacher held class outside, and the first order of business was to run laps around the track. Ally was a thin, muscular girl. As soon as their feet hit the loose gravel, Bernadette realized the flaw in their plan. She was going to have trouble keeping up with Ally.

Ally noticed Bernadette lagging and slowed her pace. "I do this every day," she said.

"You're on the track team?"

"No way. Running is boring. I've been taking gymnastics since I was four. We run to build endurance." It was working, Bernadette thought. Ally didn't have any difficulty talking while she loped alongside. Bernadette would have to disguise her panting by asking short, open-ended questions.

"You run every day?"

"Well, Monday through Saturday. And weight lifting, too," Ally said. "It sounds intense, but I got the Olympic Dream"—she used both hands to make quote marks in the air—"and got used to it. Now I don't want to do the Olympic thing, but I still like the routine."

"Wow, the Olympics?" Bernadette puffed out between breaths. "You must be good."

"Actually, there are girls in my club now who are better than me. Once I thought I would rather die than not be a gymnast, but then I found out I like to eat. Coaches are always hinting that gaining weight is not a good thing if you have the Olympic Dream. My mother was not into that," Ally said.

"That was sensible of you."

"No, I wasn't sensible. I was sick. My mother realized that before I did. Now I still work out, but my goal is the varsity team at high school, and a college scholarship."

Bernadette wondered what Ally meant by "sick," but she didn't want to pry. After they ran two laps, they joined the rest of the class, which had gathered around the gym teacher. Bernadette listened as he explained different track-and-field events. He wanted everyone to try the long jump, a sprint, the hurdles. . . . Bernadette turned to ask Ally which event she wanted to do first, but when she looked to her right, where Ally had been standing, Ally wasn't there. Then she looked down. Ally was bent over backward, pressing her weight onto her hands and shoulders, lifting her feet off the ground one at a time.

"Ouch. Does that hurt?"

"You've never done a backbend? It's a great stretch. C'mere, I'll spot you."

"My back would snap in half."

"No, it won't."

Ally put her hands lightly on Bernadette's lower back. "Bend."

"I can't."

"Yes, you can. Don't worry. I'm stronger than I look."

Bernadette tipped her head backward and instinctively closed her eyes. Blood rushed to her brain, and she saw spots on a midnight-blue field. She could feel Ally's hands supporting her back.

"Keep going," Ally said.

"I can't!"

"You can. Just let go."

The deep backward bend made the muscles in Bernadette's abdomen scream. Her head felt swimmy, but she reached with her hands until she felt cold, wet grass and hard pebbles pressing into her palms. She had closed her eyes, and when she opened them now, the world was upside down.

"How do I get up?!" she shouted, feeling a small panic.

"You did it, see?"

Bernadette collapsed onto the grass. "Gosh, that is a great stretch."

"It gets easier. You have to trust me. And yourself." Ally spotted Bernadette several times until Bernadette could do it by herself. Then Ally helped her kick her legs up into a brief handstand before landing on her feet again. The first few times, Bernadette's arms failed her and she collapsed, suddenly, like an ironing board put away for storage, but by the end of class she could do what Ally called a back walkover with a boost from Ally. Bernadette made a secret resolution to take yoga when she became a grown-up again. The night before she had read a book on "metaphysical vision questing," a process of meditation, proper breathing, and yoga poses that would allow you to revisit parts of your life that needed "correcting" or "resolution." Bernadette finished the book certain it contained nothing of help for her particular problem, but the book jacket said the author was sixty, and in her photo she looked lean, fit, and no more than thirty-five. So Bernadette had put some stock in the yoga part of it.

"See, you actually learned something in gym," Ally said as they headed back to the building. "Can you do a cartwheel?"

"I used to be able to."

"Did you used to work out?"

"A long time ago."

"Elementary school?"

"Right."

"Well, try one now. Your body doesn't forget."

Mine has, Bernadette thought. "You do it first. I'll watch."

Ally's cartwheels were things of beauty. She looked like the big front wheel of an old locomotive, spokes turning in slow measures. Bernadette was clumsy, but she was able to put weight on her arms and get turned around in the air.

"That was pretty awful," Ally said, laughing. "Do it again." Bernadette and Ally did cartwheels all the way back to the locker room. Ally was laughing at how dizzy Bernadette was getting, and Bernadette was laughing because being dizzy was a funny feeling. It reminded her of little kids who spun themselves around like helicopter blades until they fell down. Why is it no longer fun to feel dizzy once you grow up? she wondered.

"You got the hang of that pretty quick," Ally said. "You should join the gymnastics team."

"You have to be kidding," Bernadette said.

"No—I mean, you won't be a starter, but there are girls who work out and perfect a routine until the coach thinks they're ready for competition," she said.

"Hey—does the team do any fund-raising? You know, like selling candy bars?" Bernadette asked.

"Gymnasts selling candy bars? No way. Last year we sold these pretty scented candles. People bought them for Hanukkah and Christmas gifts," Ally said. "But the selling is voluntary. Coach always says if it makes you uncomfortable, don't do it."

"When does the team start practicing?"

"Next week, but we don't have our first meet until after the holiday break," Ally said.

"Okay, I'll do it."

"Great!" They had reached the locker room before Bernadette realized she had totally lost track of Victoria Cavendish.

PATRICK

TUESDAY, OCTOBER 13

Patrick got an A on his immigration report, and Mr. Posnak had written across the top, *Excellent job.*

"The papers were not uniformly good," Mr. Posnak said, threading himself through the aisles handing back papers, "but there was one that was a model of oral history amplified by research."

Arrrrgh, don't let it be mine, Patrick thought, knowing if it was, he would never hear the end of the phrase "model of oral history." He didn't dare look over at Kyle.

"Patrick, would you please share your report with the rest of the class?" Mr. Posnak asked.

"You mean read it?"

"Correct."

"Do I have to?"

"No. If you don't, I will."

Oh, that's worse, Patrick thought. He'll make it sound dramatic. "Can I sit right here?"

"Yes, but please read loud enough so that everyone can hear."

Patrick had turned the paper over so nobody would see his grade. He flipped it back now and folded down the top corner to cover the A. He liked getting good grades, but he didn't want anyone to think he did.

" 'My Mother's Roots,' " he began. It should have been subtitled "According to My Father," since his mother had never responded to his e-mail. His father had to fill in a lot of blanks.

My mother is a first-generation Irish-American, which means that she, like millions of others, is the daughter of two people who left Ireland and moved to America in the twentieth century.

Her father was from County Clare, the son of farmers. Her mother was from County Kerry, the daughter of farmers.

I never met my grandfather, but my grandmother was alive until this past March, and she lived just a mile from my house. She was an interesting person, although she was not your normal grandmother. Before she married, her name had been Looney and she would tell us, proudly, that meant she was half Looney. And she was.

"That makes you a little Looney, too, McBride," came a voice from behind him, and the class laughed. Even Mr. Posnak chuckled.

"Is that enough?" Patrick asked, looking at the teacher.

"Keep going, you're doing great," Mr. Posnak answered.

My grandmother grew up in a part of the country that she said the British never fully colonized, which means that they didn't thoroughly wipe out Irish customs or Gaelic, which is the Irish language, although they tried. The British had occupied parts of Ireland since Oliver Cromwell was in power in the seventeenth century. My grandmother would tell you Oliver Cromwell was archenemy No. 1 of the Irish people. According to the encyclopedia, he was a British military leader who gave away a lot of Irish land to his officers.

The Looneys were not rich. I've been to the house my grandmother grew up in, and the bathroom is outside in a shack and they don't have a telephone or a television. But they did own land, lots of land, and it was fertile. It is beautiful even if you don't like scenery. It looks like a quilt made of different shades of green and gold. You can stand on the back steps of my great-grandfather's house, and everything you can see around you is his. There are no buildings, so you can see a long way.

My grandmother's family grew potatoes, onions, and peat, which they used for fuel. They had a barn full of cows. The family would take what they needed for milk and butter. Whatever was left over, one of her brothers would cart each morning to sell at the creamery in town.

But like a lot of other Irish families, my grandmother's family was large. She was the seventh of eight children. My grand-uncle Declan is the oldest. He got the farm when my great-grandfather died. Five of the eight children came to America.

In Ireland it is common for people to leave. By the time my grandmother left, a lot of people had been leaving for a hundred years. They began leaving in big numbers when a germ got on the potato crop. According to the encyclopedia, from 1845 to 1849, the whole crop was wiped out. It was "one of the worst natural disasters in recorded history." Hundreds of thousands of people starved to death, or died of cholera or typhoid, which are diseases. Hundreds of thousands of others left the country. According to the U.S. Census, which I found at www.census.gov, 1.6 million Irish people emigrated to America in the ten years following the potato famine.

Some of my grandmother's ancestors were among these immigrants—but if you owned land, somebody stayed to tend the farm, and my grandmother is a descendant of those Looneys. Over the next century, however, many of her other ancestors left for America, not, she would say, because it was the land of opportunity, but because Ireland didn't offer much to young people. My grandmother left when she was twenty. A boat took her from a place called Galway to New York, past Ellis Island and the Statue of Liberty. She told me she cried the whole way, missing her mother and father. She married my grandfather, Brendan Downey, who she met on the boat. They lived in Queens for a while, then bought a home here in North Massapequa. They had four children. Their youngest child is my mother.

Who has also left, Patrick thought. "Do I have to read the rest of it?"

"No, that's great. Thank you, Patrick," Mr. Posnak said. "You know, I didn't think of it until you read that paragraph aloud right now, but there's a girl named Downey in one of my other classes who just came here from Ireland. You might want to talk to her to find out if you two share an ancestry. Now, does anyone want to comment on Patrick's paper?"

The class was quiet. Mr. Posnak launched into what he liked about Patrick's paper—the blend of primary sources and research, *documented* research, he was saying, when Patrick tuned out. He folded the report in half and tucked the sheets into his notebook. With the notebook cover shielding it, he read the rest of what he had written, but only to himself:

I think, unlike a lot of immigrants, my grandmother never tried to become an American. When you went to her house, it was like going to another country. She didn't do things the way other people do. She never put ice in drinks. She never had Coke or normal snacks. She never made me hot chocolate, although she did teach me how to make a fire. She knew how to find things in the woods—certain bugs, and plants that bloomed only at a certain time of day. She let me help her bake—bread and cakes and stuff—and she let me work in her garden. She had a big garden—that was her hobby. She planted potatoes and I would dig them up. She never cared how dirty I got. She liked dirt and she loved potatoes. She would say her potato crop was the only part of her that ever sank roots. I never knew what she meant by that until I did this paper.

Rereading the last paragraph, Patrick was suddenly thrilled that Mr. Posnak had made him reread the paper. He had been totally stalled in his search for his mother. But the words about his grandmother's garden had jogged his memory just now. He remembered something else she had planted there: an extra key to her house.

BERNADETTE

THURSDAY, OCTOBER 15

Halfway through October, a warm wind whisked leaves from the trees, their branches scantily clad in brilliant bronze and vivid yellow. The sun shone down like a spotlight from high above the clouds.

"Let's eat outside," Donna suggested, so Bernadette and Annmarie got a table while Donna and Judy went through the lunch line. The picnic tables were covered with gray splotches dropped by birds.

"I'll go get a rag," Bernadette said, "if you'll hold my things." Annmarie held out her hands to take the lunch bag and book.

When she came back out, Patrick, the Baxter twins, and another boy Bernadette didn't know were sitting at the picnic table next to them. Patrick was laughing. His bangs had gotten long. He looked like a pony, right down to his long knobby-kneed legs, stretched out under the picnic table, crossed at the ankles.

It's warm, but not warm enough for shorts, Bernadette

was thinking. She didn't realize she was staring until Annmarie's voice pulled her out of her reverie.

"He's cute."

"Who?" Bernadette asked, feigning surprise.

"Patrick McBride—isn't that who you're looking at?"

"Oh, no, I was daydreaming. Do you smell chocolate?" Bernadette tried to steer the topic in a different direction.

"It's my lip gloss. Don't worry. Your secret's safe with me," Annmarie said, winking at Bernadette and nudging her with an elbow. "It is sad about his mother, though."

"What about his mother?"

"You don't know? She's missing. It was in the newspaper."

"In the newspaper? When?"

"A while ago. I didn't read it. My mother did. My mother thinks something bad must have happened to her, otherwise somebody would have heard from her by now."

"Something bad? Like what?"

"Like killed by a lunatic, probably."

Bernadette's body quaked involuntarily. Me. Killed. People think I'm dead. Am I dead? Maybe I have been reincarnated, she thought. She had just finished an entire book on reincarnation, but she still considered the idea ridiculously optimistic.

"Fish sticks, yuck," Donna said, plunking her tray down on the table. "The food here gets worse every day. If you're a vegetarian, there is virtually nothing to eat." To Bernadette's relief, the conversation made a sharp turn to food. Donna and Annmarie engaged in a breathless rant about the evils of beef.

Bernadette was quiet, her thoughts fixed on her own suspected death. She wondered which was worse: the fact that

Patrick might believe she was dead, or that he seemed wholly unfazed by it.

"Detta, are you okay?" Donna asked, bursting her trance. "You look like a ghost."

"I don't feel good, actually. I think I'll go to the nurse."

"You want us to walk you there?" Annmarie asked.

"No, I'm okay. Just queasy." Bernadette bunched up the rest of her sandwich in its aluminum-foil wrapping and put it in her paper bag. "See you guys later."

"Hope you feel better," they chorused as Bernadette tossed her paper bag in the trash and waved. She managed a weak smile before turning to head back into the building.

Bernadette slipped out a side door that opened onto the parking lot and threaded her thin frame between cars until she reached the chain-link fence that bordered the school property. She climbed it and ran through a backyard.

She was worried about going to the library because she thought somebody might ask her why she wasn't in school, but her need to know what had been in the newspaper outweighed her worry. She knew where the back copies of the newspapers were, so she headed right there, her head high, pretending to have confidence she didn't actually possess.

She had to leaf back several weeks before she found the story. She had mixed feelings upon learning that her colleagues knew less about her disappearance than she did. *Investigators . . . found no signs of foul play.* Maybe she wasn't dead, then. This gave her comfort.

She flipped forward through the pages again and found a two-paragraph update she had missed on her first pass. It said even less, basically just repeating the request for information.

She walked home, her head full of worries. Did Gerard and the boys assume she was dead? Patrick hadn't even missed a day of school. She should have called them. But what would she say? I'm okay, but a lot shorter? They wouldn't even have recognized her voice.

What *had* happened to her? She had read through most of the stack of the books she had brought home, and she was no closer to understanding, never mind finding a way to undo it. She felt tears coming on.

And what about her mother? She was mixed up in this, too.

That's the key, Bernadette thought. My mother. I should have confronted her right away, but it had been so wonderful to see her and spend time with her again. And she had weighed her options—confront her family? go to the police? stay in bed until she woke up in the right body?—and concluded the best thing to do was to keep going to school so she would see Patrick and walking by the house to look in on the other two boys. They did all seem to be fine, although Kevin had cut his hair impossibly short. She had wondered if he had gotten interested in competitive swimming.

Now she would *have* to talk to her mother, even though it didn't seem like she knew what was going on either. Maybe she knew of some antidote—an *aging* potion. Then a thought stopped her cold.

If I do go back to my own family, what happens to my mother? Does she go back to wherever she was? It was too scary to think about. Bernadette felt a headache coming on.

Lost in thought, she wasn't looking up when she turned right onto the cul-de-sac, but something flashy caught her eye, and when she saw what it was, she froze. Outside her mother's home, there was a police car parked at the curb, its blue lights twirling silently, and a police van parked in front of the neighbors'. Circling her car, which had been parked in the driveway since the night before her birthday, there was a long yellow ribbon of plastic tape, the kind police string around crime scenes. The strobe lights on top of a tow truck threw beams of ocher light across the pavement as it backed up to her station wagon. Bernadette stared at the scene, immobilized, until a coal-black rabbit hopped nearly across her shoes, startling her. Then she fled.

PATRICK

THURSDAY AFTERNOON,
OCTOBER 15

Patrick walked home from school, thinking out his plan for the next day. He had decided to wait until Friday, when the baby-sitter, Mrs. Compton, was on duty, to go by his grandmother's to look for the house key. Mrs. Compton was a lot fuzzier on precisely what time he was supposed to be home than Brent was. You couldn't get away with being an hour late with Brent, and he had been there Tuesday *and* Wednesday already this week, because Mrs. Compton's Maltese was having dental surgery.

Patrick was sure he remembered where the key was. His grandmother had white, concrete circles arranged like a tic-tac-toe grid crisscrossing the garden so she could weed, seed, water and harvest without trampling her plants. The key was directly beneath the fourth white circle from the left side in the third row. He could picture a worm curling around its brassy notches right now, because when he had lifted those stones in the past, there were always a few worms beneath them. Patrick couldn't understand why a worm would choose to have all that weight on top of it. Why didn't it crush them?

Once he found the key, he would take a quick tour of the house. He didn't know what he was looking for, but maybe being in the last place his mother had been would provide a clue, some new direction he could follow.

When he got home, he showed the immigration paper to Brent, who was listening to Neil read aloud. Neil was fixated on Amelia Bedelia. Today's story was about Amelia playing baseball. Boy, there's a happy marriage of Neil's interests, Patrick thought. Brent looked at the paper and a smile broke across his face. Brent smiled easily, big wide grins showing straight white teeth. It was impossible not to smile back at a smile like that.

"The pitcher threw the ball," Neil read. Brent put his hand in the air, palm out, and Patrick joined it with a hard clap.

"The batter hit it," Neil continued. Patrick and Brent laughed. Kevin looked up from the table, where he was doing a math crossword puzzle, the kind where if you get one answer wrong, it makes the other answers wrong, too. He was doing it in ink, Patrick noticed.

Patrick gestured to Brent that he was going upstairs. Brent nodded and his attention went back to Neil and Amelia.

Patrick went into his mother's office and turned on the computer. He had homework, but he needed a break, so he played Mario Brothers.

He was upstairs for an hour or more before he heard Kevin calling him, then heard him bounding up the stairs.

"Patrick!" Kevin burst in. "Turn the TV on." Kevin dashed into his parents' bedroom and grabbed the remote from the top of the set.

"Lemme guess. The strippers don't like their makeovers?" Patrick asked, turning back to the computer screen.

"C'mere!" Kevin said, and the urgency in his voice caught Patrick's attention. He walked down the hallway to his parents' room. "Look," Kevin said, pointing to the TV. "That's Grandma's house."

Patrick stared at the screen. It *was* his grandmother's house, and there was a reporter from the cable news channel standing in front of it, a strand of yellow tape behind her.

"Turn it up!"

The picture of the reporter disappeared, and the next picture showed a tow truck, moving away with a Volvo station wagon.

"That's Mom's car," Patrick said. The reporter was saying, "Evidence technicians will search the vehicle for signs of a struggle. . . ."

"Patrick, Brent says you're up," Neil said, standing at the threshold of the room. "What're you guys watching?"

Kevin hurriedly switched off the TV. "Just the news."

BERNADETTE

LATE AFTERNOON,
THURSDAY, OCTOBER 15

Bernadette spent the remainder of daylight in hiding, scared of the scene outside her mother's home, scared to venture into town, scared to think.

She backed away from the street quickly, strode down the next one without glancing at the homes on either side, afraid to catch someone's eye or attention, and cut through a backyard into the same woods that backed up to her mother's house. Fifty yards beyond the line of trees there was the bike path that cyclists and joggers used. When she was young, she and her mother had taken long walks there. Her mother knew the names of all the plants and would often suggest a hike when she was low on a wildflower or weed she used for making poultices or headache cures. Fiona prided herself on minimizing her contact with doctors. Bernadette's father would complain that they had medical insurance—why wasn't she using it?—but Fiona put far more store in nature than in man.

Bernadette walked with her hands in front of her face after stumbling into a sticky web stretched between two trees, but reached the bike path without upsetting another spider's handiwork. She headed away from her mother's house, her feet crushing a carpet of fallen leaves. She had no place to go, so she dawdled, looking around and down, searching the ground cover on both sides of the path for wild blooms and sleeping fairies, who, her mother said, often used empty acorn shells for beds. The October sun had coaxed the oxeye daisies and aster out for their last show of the season, and the woods were freckled with white and purple flowers.

Bernadette had her backpack and in it, her flute and a paperback copy of *Little Women,* a book she had forgotten how much she liked, having not read it in about twenty-five years. She would have liked to practice her flute—she was having trouble with her right pinkie—but she didn't want anyone to know she was there, so she sat with her back against an oak tree and opened the book. *Little Women* was a lot more enjoyable to read than anything in the paranormal stack, which she had finished without learning a single thing about her condition. Ants marched over her corduroys and she wished she hadn't thrown her lunch away, but it was easier to surrender herself to Jo's troubles than to think about her own. She got to the part where Meg feels lonely because her obsession with her newborn twins has caused her husband to seek adult conversation elsewhere. Bernadette chuckled over how little had changed in 150 years.

Bernadette figured it was late afternoon, past four o'clock, because she got company in the woods. First, two mothers, the arms of their sweaters knotted around their waists, chatting while their little boys ran ahead, collecting rocks and tree branches longer than they themselves were tall. They made her think of Patrick and Kevin when they were small boys. They had been great playmates for each other. When had their interests diverged? she wondered. Was it when Patrick started school?

Then came the power walkers and the joggers, mostly women, with their headsets and fanny packs and water bottles. Bernadette knew a lot of people came here to exercise, though it was a place she had consigned to childhood memory. What a mistake, she thought. Not wanting to attract attention, she kept reading without looking up, stealing glances at the parade after it had passed her.

When she felt sure by the angle of the sun that it was close to twilight, she headed back toward her mother's house. She wanted to see the house from the street to be sure the sheriff's department had gone before she went in the back door, so she walked to a spot where the path emptied onto a paved street and then backtracked through the neighborhood. As she suspected, the police had left, though the neighbors were now all home. To avoid them, she retraced her steps, back to the bike path and through the woods. It was full dark by that time, but for the light from a sliver of the moon, and she had to guess which house was her mother's. She chose the house that had only one light on, crossing her fingers in hopes it was the right one.

She walked into another spiderweb picking her steps up to the yard, but she had guessed correctly. Beyond the trees was her mother's garden, now just a small square of fall vegetables and a plot of poreens, as her mother called them—fall potatoes that never grew bigger than the size of a hen's egg. Bernadette could pick out the cement circles that led through the yard to the back door.

Her mother was waiting for her in the kitchen, tea cooling in a porcelain cup. Bernadette, exhausted, famished, and wanting a shower to rid herself of sticky spider silk, opened the door softly, not knowing what to expect. Her mother's eyes met hers, but neither said anything immediately.

Her mother raised her cup to her lips and blew across the steam. "You better tell me what's going on, Bernadette."

"About the police?"

"Is there something else?"

"No. Didn't you talk to them?"

"Oh, no, I made myself scarce."

"I'm not sure I can explain it," and from her question, Bernadette knew her mother couldn't explain what was going on either.

Fiona took another sip of tea, but her eyes stayed firm on Bernadette. "This came from the school." She pushed a white envelope across the kitchen table. "The police must have brought it in, otherwise I never would have seen it. No mail comes here these days."

"What is it?" Bernadette said, twirling the envelope around to face her.

"Some kind of report card."

Bernadette felt a secret thrill. Having been an uneven student the first time around, she was excited about this one. It was a single sheet, marked "Interim Report." There were two columns, one that listed the classes she was taking and another titled "Projected First Quarter Grade." Bernadette looked at the string of A's—straight A's!—and couldn't help but smile.

"Did you read it?" she asked, shrugging off her backpack.

"It was addressed to me—or to the mother of you, I should say." She paused to take another sip of tea. "I'm wondering what kind of magic you're using."

"Magic?" Bernadette unbuttoned her coat and looped it over the shoulders of a chair. "I don't know any magic."

"A in social studies. A in language arts, whatever that is. A in science. For God's sake, there's an A in math. You've never done better than a C-plus before."

This was not the reaction Bernadette was hoping for. Her stomach let out a loud grumble.

"You make it sound like I've done something wrong," Bernadette said, moving to the refrigerator, studying the contents. Have I done something wrong? she wondered. The events of that last night ran through her head as they had dozens of times since her birthday: I *kidded* Gerard about making me much younger. I drank a glass of liquid from the pantry. I toasted my mother and youth. I went to bed. How is what happened my fault?

"I've a suspicious mind, Bernadette. Brilliance doesn't happen overnight, nor to a girl who rarely cracks her textbooks. Truth be told, with the time you've been spending skating and playing the flute, I was expecting worse news than I'm accustomed to getting when these things arrive."

What could she tell her? That math made a lot more sense after years of keeping a budget and balancing a checkbook? That her original revulsion at science—dissecting frogs? gross!—seemed a tad silly after she had given birth by C-section?

"Is there anything to eat?"

"You've not been in my pantry, have you, Bernadette?"

"What's in the pantry?" Bernadette was not sure this was the moment to bring up the *Forrior Geraugh* Cure.

The kettle whistled, and Fiona lifted the tea bag from her saucer and dunked it in her empty cup. "I see you're getting very smart," she said, standing to answer the kettle and refill her cup. "I'm warning you, Bernadette. Don't play with spirits. Here," she said, reaching into a wooden bowl on the counter. "Have an apple."

PATRICK

THURSDAY, OCTOBER 15

Patrick heard his father's car pulling into the driveway.

"Dad's home," Patrick said, and Neil went scurrying downstairs.

"You think we're going to get some info?" Kevin asked him. He had turned the television back on after Neil left the room, but the newscaster was now chatting with the weather lady.

"Let's go find out," Patrick said.

When his father came in the front door, Patrick noticed how gaunt he looked. Maybe he wasn't eating enough fruit. His mother was always ragging on his father to eat better, but his father was tall and thin and could plow through a whole box of doughnuts at a sitting.

"Neil, buddy—go on outside and shoot some hoops with Brent for a couple of minutes, okay? You and I have to go to the store soon," his father said. Then he turned to Patrick and Kevin.

"Have a seat, guys," Dad said, gesturing to the living room. "I'll be right with you."

Patrick and Kevin exchanged an anxious glance. Kevin slumped into the couch. Patrick sat down on the arm of a chair.

Patrick could hear the water running in the kitchen, and then his father reappeared, drying his glasses on a dishtowel. The purple crescents beneath his eyes were more pronounced than usual and his skin looked pale.

"Grandma's house was on TV," Kevin said.

"It was?" He clearly hadn't thought of that. He put his glasses back on and sat across from the boys, on the brick steps of the fireplace. "Okay. Let me tell you what I know. It may not be what you heard on TV."

Patrick was bracing for the worst. He was determined he would not cry, though his mother would have told him it was fine to cry.

"I just came from the police station. It seems that somebody has withdrawn money from our checking account using your mother's ATM card."

"So somebody stole her wallet," Patrick said. A huge wave of relief washed over him, and he slid from the arm of the chair into the cushion.

"That's right."

Kevin was sober. "Yeah, but who took the wallet? And don't you need a password, Dad?"

"That's right, too, Kevin," he said.

"So do we still think she's just taking a break?" Kevin asked.

Patrick watched as his father removed his glasses and rubbed his eyes. He took a deep breath. "No, Kevin, this doesn't answer all our questions. I don't know what it means. I wanted you to hear about it from me, because I talked to Mom's boss, and they'll have a story in the paper tomorrow. The newspaper is going to offer a reward for information."

"A reward?" Patrick asked. "She's not a criminal!"

"No, a reward to anybody who might know where she is. Listen, I don't think Neil is ready to hear any of this, so I don't want either of you to mention it to him. Somebody at school might, but I've talked to his teacher so she'll know how to handle it. I'm going to talk with him myself when I figure out what to say."

"We're not going to say anything," Patrick answered, looking sideways at Kevin, who was staring off into space.

"I appreciate that. I'm going to call Aunt Claire," his father announced, putting his hands on his thighs, pushing himself up. His mother's relatives had been calling frequently and Patrick sensed his father was frustrated by not having anything to tell them. Kevin and Patrick sat in silence while they listened to their father leave a message on their aunt's answering machine. He appeared again in the living room.

"I'm going to go to the grocery store. I'll take Neil," he said, jingling his keys in his pocket. "Any special requests?"

They both said no. They were quiet until they heard the car backing down the driveway.

"She's not coming back," Kevin said.

"Give it a rest, Kevin," Patrick answered angrily, before he even looked at Kevin. He was immediately sorry he said it—there were tears in Kevin's eyes. Kevin—Mr. Cool, his father called him—never cried.

"Patrick, get real. Where is she? Our mother! Do you

think she wandered off to party for a while? Something's happened to her. Something bad. The next conversation we're going to have like this with Dad is when they find her body!"

"Don't say that!"

Kevin put his head in his hands and began to weep. Big, body-racking sobs. Patrick moved closer to him. He let him cry. After a few minutes, he put his arm around him.

"Kevin, she is coming back. I know it."

"How do you know it?" he shouted, throwing off Patrick's arm. His eyes were red, his cheeks wet.

"I can't explain it, but I feel like she's near," Patrick said quietly. He did feel that, not at home so much as at school. What he couldn't say to Kevin—couldn't say because it sounded too ridiculous—was that he was going to find her.

"You're living in a fantasy, Patrick." Kevin elbowed him away.

"You watch too much TV."

"And you don't watch enough."

Foul Play Suspected in Reporter's Disappearance

FARMINGDALE—The Nassau County Sheriff's Department has opened a criminal investigation into the disappearance of Bernadette McBride, 40, wife of Dr. Gerard McBride and a *Newsday* reporter, after learning money was withdrawn from the couple's bank account at a local ATM earlier this week.

McBride has not been seen since September 7, when she left her home shortly after 7 P.M., headed for the unoccupied home of her late mother. Gerard McBride said he alerted authorities earlier this week after learning that someone had withdrawn money from the couple's checking account.

"It doesn't mean it wasn't Mrs. McBride who took the money out, but it raises our suspicions that somebody else is perhaps involved," Sgt. Robert Murray said.

Murray said the withdrawal took place on October 1 at an ATM outside the Pathmark supermarket on Carmans Road. He said detectives decided to open a criminal investigation of McBride's disappearance after a review of the surveillance tape showed that whoever withdrew the money apparently knew to stand deliberately out of range of the machine's camera.

"We've seen this happen before where the culprit actually kneels down and reaches up to make the transaction so the camera only gets the top of his head," Murray said.

The withdrawal was made during daylight hours. Anyone who saw suspicious activity at the ATM that day is asked to call the Crime Stoppers hotline at 1-800-577-TIPS.

On Thursday, the sheriff's department impounded McBride's 1994 Volvo station wagon, which had been parked outside her mother's house on William Street in North Massapequa, since her disappearance. Though the vehicle did not appear to have been tampered with, Murray said evidence technicians would search the vehicle.

A search of the North Massapequa house did not turn up McBride's wallet or personal belongings, leading investigators to believe that whoever used the ATM card also has information about McBride's whereabouts. The house showed no sign of forced entry.

McBride, the mother of three boys, has been a *Newsday* employee since 1985. Her occasional column, "Family Matters," appears in the Living section.

Newsday is offering a $10,000 reward for anyone with information about the case.

BERNADETTE

FRIDAY, OCTOBER 16

On Friday, Donna insisted Bernadette go ice skating with them that night.

"My mother will pick you up. Where do you live?"

That is the last thing I need, Bernadette thought. Donna's mother knocking on the door of a dead woman's house, looking for the twelve-year-old girl who lives there.

Plus, she had gotten the fund-raising materials from the gymnastics team, and she was planning to ring the doorbell at her family's house late that afternoon—after Gerard had gotten home—and trying to calculate a way to get herself invited inside. She had decided she would pretend to have left her pen at the last house she visited.

"Well, actually, I have a few things to do after school. Can I meet you at your house?"

"Sure. Give me your notebook—I'll draw you a map. Where will you be coming from?"

"The library." It wasn't actually a lie. Bernadette did plan to go to the library after school. She was hoping there would be a story explaining why the sheriff's department had been outside the house, and she quickly found it once she got there. Her disappearance had moved up to page 3. Her heart sank when she read about the ATM. How stupid! she thought. Of course Gerard would think someone had stolen my card. She puzzled over the part about deliberately standing *out of range of the machine's camera*. She had done no such thing. Could the camera have missed her because she was so short? Could she begin a brilliant life of crime now that she had this information?

She found a chair in a back corner of the library and unzipped her book bag. She had finished *Little Women* the night before, so she had plucked a book from the bookcase in the living room as she ran out the door that morning. *Irish Popular Legends* by Cornelius T. Murphy. She wasn't due at Donna's until 6:30, so she planned to read until the library closed at five o'clock, then try to sell her family a scented candle. What if they said no? They might. She tried to imagine Gerard buying a scented candle, and couldn't.

Bernadette was deep into her book on Irish folklore when the loudspeaker crackled with the announcement that the library would close in fifteen minutes. She had just finished a chapter, so she closed the book and ran her hand over the green fabric cover. She flipped it open to find the copyright date, which was 1935. She couldn't picture her mother buying this book and realized Fiona had probably brought it with her when she left Ireland. No doubt it had sat on a shelf for decades without Bernadette ever noticing it, but now she felt it explained so much about her mother and her eccentric ways. She had thought her mother was old-fashioned. It was much more than that. The chapter she had just finished was on folk medicine. It listed various herbs, cures, and customs, and the medicinal value people believed them to have. She flipped back to it, rereading:

Of all superstitions, the medical lingers the longest. The medicine men believe firmly in the efficacy of their art and often refuse payment for its exercise. Of course, what was science—written, acknowledged, and accepted science— two centuries ago is now pronounced vulgar error and popular superstition. Yet the practice of it continues unabated in the countryside, despite the introduction and availability of modern methods.

Her mother was two centuries out of date. She still not only believed in all these natural remedies, she employed them, and to the best of Bernadette's recollection, most of them worked! She remembered as a child being made to drink vile potions her mother mixed up. But she also remembered that they made her stomachaches and headaches much easier to bear.

Another chapter explained the tradition of May Eve bonfires, held on April 30, to welcome the onset of warmer weather, and this, too, was a practice she was now sure her mother had quietly, but rigidly, adhered to. The book said the custom was to carry an ember from the bonfire and use it to kindle a fire at home. Such a fire would protect a family from witchcraft. If the ember died before rekindling a fire, it was an omen of misfortune. Even the ashes from fires kindled by May Eve embers were considered good luck. Mothers would sew a teaspoon of them into the clothing of a child about to cross the Atlantic. Bernadette wondered if her mother had come to America with ashes from her family's kitchen fire in the hem of a dress. She had a memory of her mother gathering the dead stalks from her garden every fall and saving them in a pile to burn off in the backyard each spring. She hadn't known it was a ritual that occurred each year on a specific date.

Bernadette put the book in her backpack and shrugged the bag over her shoulders. As she took her usual route toward the house where her family lived, she wondered if the boys knew about the newspaper article. She was sure they did. After all, she had heard about the other story from Annmarie. Certainly, someone would have mentioned it to Kevin or Patrick even if they hadn't seen it at home.

When she turned down Jackson Avenue, she could see Neil playing in the driveway. She missed Neil and his rascal ways more than anything. Oh, heck, she missed them all—the noise, the wrestling, the messes, the wisecracking, everything. Sometimes, she felt an actual physical ache. But Neil probably missed her more than the others did. Despite his hero worship of his brothers, despite his wide circle of playmates, despite his ever-increasing ability to do things for himself, he was her baby.

As she got closer to the house, Bernadette could see he was playing basketball in the driveway with Jessica, who lived two doors down. She was the same age as Neil but a head taller than he was. Bernadette loved to watch the two of them play together because she knew from experience it was only a matter of time until Neil would refuse to have anything to do with girls. Jessica was actually better suited to him than many boys his age. Like Neil, she had an endless appetite for activity.

Bernadette didn't see Kevin or Patrick, but a woman she didn't know was sitting in the porch swing—*my* porch swing! Bernadette thought—reading a magazine. Bran was sitting, disloyally, Bernadette decided, at the woman's feet, chewing on a rawhide bone. Was this a baby-sitter? What was the alternative? Gerard couldn't have replaced her already, could he?

Bernadette was across the street, about even with the house, when she heard the phone ring inside. The woman got up. "Be right back," the woman said in the general direction of the driveway, before disappearing into the dark house.

Well, if this was a baby-sitter, Bernadette would fire her immediately. I would have made Neil and Jessica come inside while I got the phone, she thought.

The candle sale would have to wait until tomorrow, although Bernadette briefly considered whether she'd have better luck getting inside the house with this inept woman in charge. But she was more interested in seeing Gerard and the boys up close than the house itself, so she decided against it. Of course this woman probably wouldn't buy a candle, Bernadette figured, so I could get two bites of the apple. No sale today, but a peek. Another crack at it tomorrow. She crossed the street. She could have a short conversation with Neil, keeping an eye on him, too, while she waited for the woman to come back out.

Jessica had slapped the basketball out of Neil's hands, but couldn't control it, and it rolled toward Bernadette's feet.

"Here you go," Bernadette said, bouncing the ball back to them. Bran had come over to sniff her and licked her hand. She scratched him behind his ears and he leaned against her legs. She immediately forgave him his previous display of disloyalty.

"Hi," Neil said, looking up at her. "You wanna play?"

"Oh, no—well, yeah, sure." Bernadette put her book bag down on the sidewalk. "How about you two against me?"

"Okay." Neil took a shot that went nowhere near the rim, and Jessica ran after the rebound. She fired a shot that hit the backboard and bounced toward the street again.

"Here, let's do a drill," Bernadette suggested, and they lined up at the edge of the driveway while Bernadette went over all the tips she could remember from having sat through countless practices with Patrick and Kevin. She picked them both up so they could dunk the ball, and they both laughed at being high enough to look down at the basket, which had been set pretty low to begin with. Her heart beat extra fast when she put her hands around Neil's waist, though she was barely strong enough to lift either of them in her shrunken state.

"What's your name?" Neil asked, his question punctuated by the sound of the screen door opening. The woman smiled at Bernadette. She had a gentle face. In fact, she looked like the type who *would* buy a scented candle—somebody who wouldn't be able to say no.

"I better go—homework," Bernadette answered, losing her nerve. "It was nice playing with you."

It was then, as she was walking down the driveway, that she saw the sign. It was tacked to the telephone pole in the right-of-way. Yellowed from the sun, its message faced the house, so it couldn't be read by passing cars or people on the other side of the street.

LOST MOM, it read, and her phone number. She forced

herself to keep walking. She wanted desperately to turn around and grab the child she knew had written this and hold him until he begged to be let go. She walked, fast, her head down, one fat tear dropping like a coin on the concrete.

She had to get home.

PATRICK

FRIDAY, OCTOBER 16

"There's a story in the paper this morning about your mother," Duffy said when Patrick met him at the corner for the walk to school.

"I know. My dad told us."

"Bummer," Duffy said, kicking a rock with his sneaker.

"Yeah," Patrick said, and kicked the rock, which had skidded into his path. He hoped Duffy would drop the subject.

"I wouldn't have brought it up, but the last time . . ." Duffy gave the rock another boot.

"It's okay. Thanks," Patrick said. The rock had bounced into the grass, and neither of them went to retrieve it. That was one of the rules. If it left the concrete, the game was over.

Patrick wasn't looking forward to the day. Because of the newspaper story, people would feel sorry for him. Teachers would pat him on the back. He seriously considered skipping school.

"Earth to Patrick." It was Kyle. "You still with us?"

"Yeah, sorry. I was thinking."

"Don't do that. Might be contagious. I asked, are you going to try out for basketball?"

Basketball. Patrick had forgotten about basketball. "Nah."

"Why not? There's openings because last year's team was a lot of eighth graders."

"I'm just not into it," he told them.

"You're not into basketball? Since when?" Kyle persisted.

"Can it, Kyle," Duffy said. "He said no."

"What are you, his mother?" Kyle said, shoving Duffy into a bush. "Oh, man, I didn't mean that, Patrick."

"Forget about it. Maybe I will try out for basketball. But my dad might not want me spending so many afternoons at school. There's a lot of stuff to do around the house," Patrick said.

"See, you dork," Duffy said. "Lay off the guy." He punched his brother in the arm. Kyle locked his arm around Duffy's neck and gave him a noogie until Duffy screamed, "Truce!" Patrick had to laugh. He wondered if Duffy and Kyle ever had a conversation that didn't end in assault.

The day passed slowly. Patrick had trouble concentrating. He stopped making eye contact with everyone after the first few people he looked at looked back at him like he was a dog tossed onto the side of the road from a moving car.

He couldn't even work up any enthusiasm for computer class. He wanted the day to end and the weekend to begin. Maybe by Monday, he would be anonymous again.

When the bell rang, he didn't wait for Duffy and Kyle. He walked straight to his grandmother's house.

He paused at the top of the cul-de-sac. There were no police cars, and someone had removed the yellow tape he'd seen on TV. The front lawn needing mowing, Patrick thought. Badly. I'll do it tomorrow, he thought.

He didn't want anyone to see him go into his grandmother's backyard, so he kept walking. He knew a back way into her yard from the bike path.

The key was where he remembered. There were no worms, but there were a few of those little steel-gray bugs that curl themselves into balls when you touch them. Remarkably, there were plants that had sprung to life on their own. Patrick had seen the yard a couple of times over the summer when he had been here with his mother, and the garden had been dry and dusty. He had been glad his grandmother wasn't around to see it looking like that.

He pried the key out of the dirt just as a small black rabbit hopped into view. It perched on its haunches, watching him.

"Looking for a snack, Mr. Rabbit?" Patrick said. "The pickings aren't as good since Grandma left, I bet."

The rabbit looked at Patrick sideways, and he noticed the curious color of its left eye—a flat blue disk. Then it cocked its head the other way, and Patrick saw its right eye, which looked greenish gray. What an odd critter, he thought. He felt the rabbit was studying him. "Don't worry, I'm not a robber," he said to the rabbit, and it bounded off, cutting a zigzag pattern through the garden until Patrick lost track of its movements.

Patrick had never used the key, but he guessed it would fit the door to the kitchen. His grandmother never used the front door. He brushed the dirt from it with his fingers, then wiped it clean against his jeans. He tried to fit it in the keyhole, but it obviously wasn't the right key.

He walked around the side of the house and was about to open the gate, so he could try it in the front door, when he saw a police car make a smooth turn into the cul-de-sac. He put the key in his pocket, shrank against the side of the house, hopped from one circle to the next, and quickly disappeared into the woods.

Tomorrow, he thought.

BERNADETTE

FRIDAY NIGHT,
OCTOBER 16

Bernadette was ice-skating, turning smooth circles around the rink, thinking about her report card and what her mother had said about the police having brought it inside. In six weeks at her mother's house, she had not seen any other mail—no letters, no magazines, no bills even. She stroked her right foot over her left, the cold air sharpening her thoughts. The loudspeaker was blaring "Candy Man," by Sammy Davis, Jr., an awful song she had not heard in years until recently, when she had heard it more than once on the radio in her mother's kitchen.

And the phone—the phone never rang either. The electricity worked, but she had kept that account open after her mother's death because she would need to have lights and heat when she began packing things up and when she put the house up for sale. But she had disconnected the telephone. She had had her mother's mail forwarded to her own address. She remembered doing these things sort of in a trance, automatically, grateful for having had something dry and procedural to do. But now Bernadette was anxious to get back to her mother's house, to check some things she hadn't thought of before, things that might help her figure out where she was, how she got there, how to get back.

"It doesn't look like anybody's home," Donna's mother said later as she pulled to the curb outside Fiona's house.

"My mother might already be in bed," Bernadette said, realizing this was a lucky break. What if her mother had been awake and waiting for her at the door? Would she introduce her? "She's an early riser."

"Do you have a key?" Mrs. Feinman wanted to know.

"I'll go around the back. The kitchen door is usually open."

"Well, wave at us so we know you got inside," said Mrs. Feinman. "Nice to finally meet you."

"Thank you for the ride. See you Monday, Donna." Bernadette gave the car door a firm push and looked back at them as she opened the gate to the yard.

The house was dark except for a light in the kitchen. She flipped a switch in the living room so the Feinmans would see her from the front window. Donna smiled and the car moved out of the cul-de-sac, trailing a stream of blue-white smoke. Bernadette released a deep breath. When they were driving home, she wondered whether Mrs. Feinman would remember that Patrick's grandmother lived on William Street. The address had been mentioned in the newspaper articles. What if she had asked about it? Bernadette would not have known what to say.

Bernadette let the curtain fall back in place and returned to the kitchen. She picked up the telephone receiver and heard what she expected she would hear: nothing. Dead air. That explained why the telephone never rang. It was amazing Donna had never asked her for her number. Now she'd have to think of something to say in case Donna did.

Next, she searched through the basket on the counter where her mother kept papers and found the report card that had come from school. DO NOT FORWARD was stamped on the envelope. RETURN IF UNDELIVERABLE. What had happened to their regular mailman? she wondered. He would have sent this back to the school. If more mail came from school, it was bound to attract notice eventually. She thought of the box of undeliverable schedules Mrs. Piazza had on her desk the first day of school.

She tiptoed upstairs and turned the light on in the hallway so she could look in on her mother. Fiona was in bed, so slight a figure buried under the covers she barely made a lump. More like a wrinkle than a hill.

Bernadette leaned over, gently resting her hand on her mother's thin shoulder. She kissed her cheek, which felt cool and smelled of pink face lotion. "I'm home," she said.

"Did you have fun?" her mother asked, not opening her eyes but covering Bernadette's hand with her own.

"Yes, it was great."

"I'm glad of it. Get some rest now. We'll talk in the morning."

"Good night," Bernadette told her, tugging up the blankets so they covered her mother's neck and pillowed at the back of her head.

She switched the hall light off and turned on a lamp in her bedroom. She pushed her door closed until it clicked shut.

She got down on her knees and quietly shook the vent loose. She had already checked to make sure the police hadn't found her hiding spot. Now she emptied her backpack of books and wedged the laptop inside. She struggled to get the zipper closed around it. While she skated, she had been trying to compose an e-mail she could send to Patrick if only she could get the laptop to work. She put her wallet in the outside pocket and propped the backpack up against her bed. She got under her covers in the clothes she had worn all day so she would not even have to dress when she awoke. She would have an unsettled night, anxious for daylight to arrive.

Saturday morning rain moved in, and a misty drizzle hung in the air. Bernadette was up early. The only repair shop she knew of was on Hempstead Turnpike, miles away. It was a long walk, and now she'd have to make sure the laptop didn't get wet. Her mother was still sleeping. She left her a note, not saying where she was going but promising to be home by lunch. She took a rain poncho from the hall closet. She could wear it over the backpack if there was a real downpour.

As she walked, she thought about what she would say if the repairman recognized that the laptop belonged to the newspaper. She had used a screwdriver to pry the metal inventory control plate from the bottom of it, but she wasn't wise to the world of stolen goods and wondered if there were other ways companies encoded their equipment to prevent it from being used by thieves. She had to run the risk. She wore her sneakers so she could escape quickly if she had to.

She got to the store before it was open, so she crossed the highway and stood under the awning of a dry cleaners.

Shortly before nine o'clock, she saw a blue Buick pull in to the repair shop and park in the back, by the Dumpster. A heavyset man with a lunch box and the newspaper tucked under one arm got out and strode toward the back of the building. A few minutes later, she saw him again, inside the shop, turning the CLOSED sign to OPEN and then unlocking the glass door at the entrance. She waited a couple of minutes, walked a half block to the traffic light, then crossed to the other side of the street.

A bell tinkled as she stepped inside the dark, cool shop. It took several seconds for her eyes to adjust. The man she had seen was already in the back, a magnifying glass on an elastic band fixed around his head, a pair of needle-nosed pliers in his thick fingers.

"Be with you in a minute," he called, not looking up from a circuit board he held.

Bernadette looked around. On every counter there were keyboards, monitors, hard drives, many of them with the entrails spilling out. There were a few working models for sale, secondhand machines the man had probably overhauled.

"What can I do for you, little lady?" he asked.

Bernadette was wrestling the laptop out of her backpack. The counter was high, almost up to her chin. She had to stand on tiptoe, holding the backpack steady with one hand while she shimmied the laptop out with the other.

"Here, I'll hold this end," the man said, holding the bottom of the backpack steady. "What's wrong with it?"

"My father says it won't turn on at all."

"Your dad's got you running his errands, huh? Could be a frayed power cord," he said, looking at the back of the laptop. "Let's try a new one."

The man reached beneath the counter and took a long black cord out of a box. He poked one end into the receptor in the laptop and the other into an outlet right on the counter. The screen flickered blue, and the machine started running through its warm-ups.

"That seemed to do the trick," he said.

Bernadette was baffled. Why didn't it work with the batteries, then, if it was a bad power cord? "How much do I owe you?" she asked.

"Well, I don't charge for flipping switches, but if you want a new power cord—see them on the rack there?" he said, pointing to the wall behind her. "Those are $49.99."

Bernadette winced at the price and got out her wallet. She started to turn to look where he was pointing, but froze when she glanced down at her wallet. In the leather slot where she had put the money from the ATM—fifteen pristine twenty-dollar-bills—there was no money. Instead, there were leaves. Flat green leaves.

"MasterCard or Visa, we take," the guy said, laughing. "Leaves, no."

Bernadette slogged home in the rain. She tried to think how the money could have been stolen. After Mrs. Piazza had seen her at the ATM, she had gone to the hardware store, the library, and then home. She had put the money in her wallet, in her bag, behind the vent. She had spent some since on groceries. She had taken out a twenty yesterday so she'd have money for ice skating, and the change from the bill was still in her pocket. But where did the rest of the money go? How did those leaves get in there?

It rained the whole way home, and Bernadette's feet were cold and aching by the time she reached the entrance to the woods. The bike path was slick with wet leaves, but the branches seemed to catch the rain, and though her pants now were sopped, she felt like less rain was falling on the backpack.

"Hello," she said, stopping on the mat in the kitchen to remove her shoes.

"Fine day to be out," her mother said. "If you're a swan."

"I had some research to do."

"Take off those clothes, child. I'll fix the tea."

Bernadette lifted the poncho straight over her head, a cascade of water falling on the linoleum. She took her pants off, too, but not the backpack. She wanted to get upstairs with it quickly. She backed out of the room, her feet chilled, her legs damp and pimply with the cold. She felt defeated.

In her room, she tried the laptop. Nothing. Apparently the battery had died at the precise moment the power cord frayed. Maybe she could borrow a power cord from someone. She wondered if Donna's parents had a laptop.

After she stowed the computer behind the vent again, she put on wool socks and dry jeans and rejoined her mother, who was in the living room with the sewing basket out and the television on.

"Your tea's on the counter, Bernadette."

"Thanks," she said, and went to get the cup. Her mother had buttered two slices of soda bread and laid them on either side of the saucer. There was something so essentially loving in the way her mother made snacks for her, and she thought about how much she liked to make sugar cookies or cupcakes for her boys—how much pleasure it gave *her* when they gobbled something down she had whipped up. She would love to be home with them now, taking a sheet of cookies from the oven, hearing Neil ask, "Are they cool enough now, Mom?" Bernadette brought the cup and saucer out to the living room so she could sit by the fire.

"What are you watching?"

"Lawrence Welk. He's got an Irish tenor on today."

"Lawrence Welk? Is he still on?"

"That's him, isn't it?"

Bernadette thought Lawrence Welk was dead, but it was Saturday afternoon. Maybe the show was a rerun. That was what she thought until the commercials came on. The first one was a political campaign ad. From the Committee to Reelect the President.

President Nixon.

Bernadette didn't say anything, but her mind worked like a microscope, her thoughts calibrating to bring the object under glass into focus.

This explained the age of the clothes in her closet.

Why that stupid Sammy Davis, Jr., song was on the radio all the time.

It wasn't just she and her mother who had been returned to 1972. It was the whole *house*. She hadn't noticed it before because there wasn't much difference between the way the house looked three decades ago and the way it looked the day her mother died. Fiona was not one for decorating or upgrading. She still had a rotary-dial phone (Patrick and

Kevin thought that was hilarious) and the same television Bernadette's father had bought so he could watch the Mets in the World Series—the *1969* World Series.

Bernadette put her teacup down and went to the kitchen. She turned on the radio. "Baby I'm-A Want You" was playing. Another moldy oldie. She turned it off and unplugged the radio.

She fished two batteries from the junk drawer, pried off the plastic door on the back of the radio, and fixed them in their slot. Then she slipped out the back door and walked to the edge of the woods.

The rain had ended, but there was still a gray pallor over everything. With her thumb she pushed the serrated edge of the radio dial until it clicked on. She kept pushing, gently, only until it got loud enough for her to hear . . . sports talk radio. No Sammy Davis, Jr., out here. Bert from Great Neck was calling on his cell phone to complain about the Jets' offense.

Now she knew why the laptop didn't work in the house. It hadn't been invented in 1972.

Back in the kitchen she returned the radio to its spot on the shelf above the sink. Her mother was still watching Lawrence Welk when she walked past her to the stairs. She quietly closed the door to her bedroom. Her mind was warning her to be patient, that this was something better done after her mother had gone to bed, but she simply couldn't wait. She got the laptop out again and stuffed it into the backpack.

"It's stopped raining. Guess I'll go for a walk," she told her mother. She did not pause for a response.

When she got to the path, she walked only a few hundred

yards before veering off to a spot behind a wide tree. She took the laptop out, dropped the backpack to the ground, and squatted on her heels. She balanced the laptop on her thighs. She flipped the switch. The laptop hummed and chimed. Then she uncurled the cord that would connect it to her cell phone and plugged that in. She said a silent prayer that no one at work had thought to cancel her cell-phone account.

She waited for the computer to finish talking to itself, then moved the cursor to the icon for e-mail. The hourglass appeared and she waited, afraid to breathe. "Please work," she whispered.

There was a pulse of blackness and then a flashing message: **Mailbox Full**, the screen read.

She quickly scanned the list. There were dozens from work, newsroom announcements automatically sent to her because, apparently, no one had taken her name off the company list just because she failed to show up for work for six weeks. But sprinkled among those, she saw at least two dozen with a different return address:

pmcbride@saltzmanms.edu

PATRICK

MONDAY, OCTOBER 19

Patrick's plans to mow his grandmother's lawn were spoiled by rain Saturday and rain Sunday. He felt like the weekend weather itself, gray and soggy. It wasn't just him, either. All four of them, cooped up in the house, had been cranky and lifeless. Kevin moped, complaining there was nothing to watch on TV, because the baseball play-offs had ended quickly and the World Series didn't start until Tuesday. Neil, who rarely cried anymore, broke down over accidentally tearing the page he had written his homework assignment on when he tried to rip it out of his notebook. His father scooped him up and rocked him like a baby. Patrick hadn't seen his father hold Neil like that in the longest time.

At least, by Monday, it did seem that people were taking less notice of him. Patrick felt he was somehow smaller, diminished, in a way, so that there was less of him to notice. Crushed, like the worms beneath a rock. He crawled through the day, and by the time he got to computer class, he felt relieved knowing that at least the day was almost over.

He depressed the button on the monitor. The lime-green light flickered and the machine turned on with a hum. His fingers found their places and pecked out *pmcbride* and his password. He always checked his mail first, though the novelty of sending messages to Kyle and Duffy had worn off because they would send back one-word messages or not write back at all.

Messages waiting: 1, the screen said.

He moved the cursor to the mailbox icon and clicked on it.

He nearly shouted out loud when he saw it, but when he tried to make a sound nothing had come out. Quickly, he read:

To: pmcbride@saltzmanms.edu
From: bmcbride@newsday.com
Subject: Your messages
Date: 10/17 12:12:24 PM Eastern Daylight Time

Patrick:

I got your messages. I only recently have been able to get my laptop to work.

I was thrilled to hear from you, though I am concerned about Kevin's head. I have long been concerned about Bun-Bun the Middle One's head, as you well know. :-)

Don't worry about any of that other stuff. I couldn't care less about the house being dirty. We'll keep the cleaning lady when I get back!

I cannot tell you where I am, but I am okay and I am working hard to get home. I need you to do me a big, big favor. Two favors. The first is, immediately after you read this message, delete it, and don't tell anybody about it. I need you to keep it secret, otherwise I might lose the ability to communicate with you this way.

Second, and this is trickier, I need you to help reassure Dad and your brothers that I'm okay. I'm not in any harm, just stuck somewhere. I know that sounds mysterious. I can't explain it yet, but maybe someday I will be able to. Can you tell them you feel in your heart that I'm okay?

I LOVE YOU. I LOVE YOU. I LOVE YOU. I LOVE YOU. That's one "I love you" for each of you. I miss all of you so much.

Remember, like *Mission Impossible,* this message will self-destruct in five seconds!

Patrick was too stunned to do anything more than blink. The teacher was talking, but it was like his ears had been shot with Novocain, the kind the dentist uses, and it had deadened them to sound. But then he heard his name, somebody whispering it from behind him, and he turned.

It was Victoria Cavendish.

"Oooooh," she was saying. "Patrick's got a girlfriend." She puckered her lips and made a high-pitched kissing sound.

Patrick panicked when he realized she was reading over his shoulder. He tried to come up with a response, but his mind froze. He was about to tell Victoria to mind her own business when he saw the girl sitting next to Victoria reach for her backpack, unzip it, and dump the contents on the floor.

"Hey, what the . . . !" Victoria shouted.

"Ladies, what's the problem?" Ms. Dobbs asked.

Patrick would thank the girl later. He swiveled around quickly and hit the delete key.

BERNADETTE

After Bernadette calmed down—Deep breaths! she told herself, conquering her intense urge to wring Victoria Cavendish's skinny neck—she realized that what Victoria had been able to read off Patrick's screen was probably just the line of "I Love You"s, written in all caps. But Bernadette had a long list of things to do, work that couldn't be done fast enough, and now she had to add getting rid of Victoria to that list.

Saturday, after she sent the e-mail to Patrick, she had taken another look at her mother's book on Irish legends. It was like a recipe book. There was a chapter on fairy charms that explained how to boil yarrow and speedwell together to create a potion that would keep devils from spoiling butter in the churn. Another charm explained how to identify your true love by placing a snail on a clean plate sprinkled with ashes or flour. The slug's color would indicate the lover's complexion, and the slimy trail it left in the grains would spell out the first initial of his name. She was having a hard time imagining a snail tracing the letter G. It'd have to be a smart snail.

But she had also pored over the section about how fairies stole humans—often by changing their appearance or the appearance of the soul they were stealing. Fairies could travel through time, make horses from straw, and carry humans into their world. Could they infiltrate the human world, too? Was that what her mother meant by her warning not to play with "spirits"? In any case, Bernadette was convinced her mother was more deeply involved in fairy magic than she had ever admitted. Of course, had she "admitted" this, who would have believed it?

The folklore book had mentioned a way of testing for the presence of fairies. Bernadette scoured the text until she finally found it, in a footnote, on page 83.

After her mother went to bed Saturday night, Bernadette had gone downstairs into the dining room. She held one glass door of the china cabinet steady while she opened the other, hoping to muffle the rattle of glass. She carefully slid out a crystal goblet—a Waterford glass her mother had gotten as a wedding gift from her own parents. She twirled it in the moonlight, sending splinters of refracted light around the dark room. Perfect, she thought.

In the kitchen, she gingerly set the glass on the counter. From the cabinet, she took down a cardboard canister of quick oats. She filled the goblet almost to the top with the grain. She covered it with a linen towel and then held the glass against her heart, her back, and each side of her waist, as the book instructed.

She put the goblet down on the counter and reread the passage.

If fairies are present, one-half of the meal will disappear at one side of the glass.

Bernadette took the cloth away. The goblet was still full.

Rats, she thought, wishing the book explained what "meal" was. Maybe Quaker Oats didn't qualify as meal. Maybe fairies don't like Quaker Oats. If she knew anything about fairies after reading her mother's book, it was that they could be picky.

Now, sitting in Language Arts on Monday, Bernadette went over her next step. She knew there was an Irish-goods shop where she might be able to find something closer to genuine Irish meal, but it was not within walking distance. During her lunch period, she had called the shop from the pay phone by the gym to make sure it would be open that afternoon. Then she phoned the train and bus station for schedule information. If she took the 2:45 P.M. bus from Carmans Road to the train station and the 3:35 P.M. train from Massapequa Park, she would make it to Merrick by four o'clock, with time to walk the few blocks to the store before it closed.

But she was running out of money. The few dollars she had left, plus all the change in her wallet, came to less than nine dollars. She had been keeping that money on her person, inside a zippered pouch, even when she went to bed, so as not to have it, too, change to leaves.

She had even dreamed one night that someone was trying to take it and woke with a start. But what she had felt was just the cold metal zipper touching her bare skin.

She would have to pay to get on the bus, but she was going to have to stow away on the train and hope "meal" didn't cost more than seven dollars. Unless the store took leaves. She had checked her wallet again Sunday night, hoping that they had turned back into cash. They hadn't.

She made the bus and the train without a problem. From Massapequa Park west to Merrick, she stayed one train car behind the conductor, crossing between cars as the train rocked westward, the rush of air blowing her backward. In Wantagh, the conductor reached the end of the train and turned around, so Bernadette stepped off the train, ran the length of the platform, and reentered the train at the far end. Her heart was beating piston-fast. Circumstances had made her a better liar, but she was still a wholly unpracticed cheat. If one of her boys was doing this, she'd be furious.

At Merrick, she rode an escalator to the street, the sun hitting her square in the eyes as she descended. She nearly ran to the shop. She'd been there before, with and for her mother, so she knew where it was.

"Good afternoon," said the woman in the shop, a slight hint of a brogue gilding her welcome. Bernadette recognized her as the owner. She was alone in the store, straightening a pile of caps into a perfect stack, like tweed pancakes.

"What can it be?" she asked. Bernadette knew what she meant was *How can I help you?* The Irish twist English in odd ways that Bernadette had always found charming. She figured they did it on purpose.

"I called earlier. I'm looking for meal. For my mother."

"Meal? Any special kind?"

"Um, well what kind do you have?"

"All types—corn, bran, and oat, fine grain or coarse—"

"Well, what's the best?"

"That depends on what you're going to use it for."

"It's a gift for my mother. She's Irish and she's always talking about 'meal good enough to tempt the fairies into showing themselves.' "

"Och! Fairy meal! You need the real stuff. Flaherty's Fine Sieve Oatmeal. It's there now, bottom shelf, next to the teas," she said, gesturing to a row of boxes at the back of the store.

The meal was $4.50 for a one-pound package, and Bernadette gripped it like gold as she traveled home the same way she had come, shaky steps taken between rattling cars moving at top speeds eastward. Fortunately, the train was now packed with commuters, and Bernadette was able to hide herself among the folds of coats and opened pages of the newspaper without any trouble.

Night was falling by the time the train pulled into Massapequa Park, but Bernadette couldn't bear to part with her last few dollars, so she walked home—miles and miles—to the entrance to the bike path on Linden Street, across the bridge over the parkway, past the turnoff to the high school, until she reached the woods that backed up to her mother's house.

Her mother called out from the living room as Bernadette entered the darkened kitchen.

"It's on the counter," she said, and Bernadette looked around in the dim light, expecting to see the usual cup of tea. Instead, she saw the goblet and the linen cloth.

Her mother knew. She knew what Bernadette was doing. Bernadette felt tremendous relief. She pulled the Flaherty's Fine Sieve Oatmeal from the sack and filled the goblet. She repeated the steps she had taken before. This time, when she removed the cloth, half the meal was gone.

"So we're enchanted, are we?" Her mother was standing in the doorway, backlit by the low lamp in the living room. She looked ethereal.

"I guess so. You didn't know that?"

"I've been addled, I'll tell you, but I think I've figured it out now. You need to get back to your family, true?"

"Is there a way?"

"Perhaps. You've got to tell me something first."

"Sure."

"Am I dead?"

Bernadette felt her eyes fill with tears.

"Technically . . . I mean . . . yes, you did die," she said. It was hard to think of her mother dead, harder still to acknowledge it aloud.

"So this is dead?" Fiona held her hands out, looking at them, as if that would help her understand. "I knew something was off, but I didn't figure it out until I saw Patrick in the garden."

"Patrick was *here*?"

"Yes, and it wasn't until I saw him that I remembered you weren't a girl anymore. I'll tell you, Bernadette. Death does powerful things to memory."

"When was he here?"

"The day you went ice-skating. It shook me so through and through, I had to take to the bed."

"Did you talk to him?"

"Oh, no. He didn't see me. But he did a curious thing. He took the key to the lock on the garden shed and tried to use it to get in the kitchen door. He's forgotten the house key is on the east side of the garden."

"I've been looking for that key!"

"For the shed? There's another one if you need it. At the bottom of the Belleek vase in the china cabinet."

"Oh, right. Boy, *living* does powerful things to the memory, too."

"You mustn't let Patrick in this house, Bernadette."

"Why?"

"I'm not sure that he wouldn't disappear."

"Because in here he hasn't been born yet?"

"Right." Fiona paused. "Bernadette, it's a delicate question, but . . . how did I die?"

"Oh, Mother, it was awful. You were in a car accident."

"I never liked those contraptions. You weren't driving, were you?"

"No. You were with Molly Brady. From church."

"Is she dead, too?"

"No, she's fine."

"Figures. She's a sturdier woman than I ever was. Okay, if that's the case, then let me ask you another question. Did you and I ever say good-bye?"

Bernadette thought back to the phone call she had gotten at work. The mad dash to the hospital, almost getting into an accident herself. The harsh lights in the emergency-room waiting area. The doctor in his green scrubs who asked her to come into a small conference room and closed the door. She could still hear the door clicking shut behind her, a sound so final she didn't have to listen to what the doctor said. She already knew. She remembered the feeling—the air going out of her lungs. The blinding headache. Then Gerard was there and she wept into his shoulder.

"No, by the time I got to the hospital, you were already gone."

Fiona moved closer and drew Bernadette into her arms. And Bernadette cried again, those same heavy sobs.

"There, there. Have a good cry, B," Fiona said. "You were always my pet."

"It's horrible to lose your mother like that," Bernadette said.

"Sure, it's horrible to lose your mother," Fiona said. "Think of how your boys feel."

"Oh, I know! You have to help me get back to them!" Bernadette pulled away so she could reach the tissue box. She drew one out and blew her nose. "I think this is all my fault because I had been tired and sad and I wished I didn't have so much to do. . . ." Bernadette couldn't continue.

"Bernadette, tell me this. I asked you this question the other day and you dodged an answer. *Have* you been in my pantry?"

"Well, I came here the night before my birthday and I took a drink from . . . here, I'll show you," Bernadette said, crossing to the pantry. She pulled the bottle holding the almond-scented liquid from its shelf.

"Och! *Forrior Geraugh!* What birthday was it?"

"My fortieth. I guess I was wishing I wasn't so old. And I was missing you. And it smelled so good. What is it?"

"It's a cure for regrets. Mixing wishes with *Forrior Geraugh* will summon the fairies, Bernadette. I thought you knew better."

"How would I have known?"

"There's a way to undo this, but you'll need help I can't give you. A body can't be pushed out of the spirit world, nor can it jump. If you want out, you must be pulled."

"Pulled?"

"There are two ways of doing it. Fairies usually carry souls off in a whirlwind. If you hear the sound of horse hooves in the wind, you can be sure that's the little people stealing a body," Fiona said.

"Well, there was a strong wind that night—so strong it blew open the front door," Bernadette remembered.

"Aye. Well, if somebody had seen you being carried off, they could've cast dust from under their feet into the whirlwind. When that happens, the fairies are obliged to release the body unharmed," Fiona said, crossing to the stove, where the kettle was already steaming. "I think we need a cup o' tea." She opened the cupboard for cups and saucers, then continued, "But it's too late for that in your case. For this problem, we'll have to use soul cakes."

"Soul cakes? I think those are mentioned in your book."

"What book?"

"This one I found in the bookcase—*Irish Popular Legends*. That's where I got the idea to test for fairies."

"Yes, you'd find a recipe for the soul cake in there. I'd forgotten I had that book. Most of it is a lot of nonsense." The kettle screeched, and Fiona turned the knob on the stove to off. "You want a cup?"

"Yes, please," Bernadette answered. "Are the soul cakes magic?"

"Magic? Oh, people think magic is some extravagant thing. You focus the mind on what you want and use nature to help. But in this case, you'll have to get someone from out there to help you," she said, nodding her head toward the front yard, the street beyond it, the town.

"Somebody who knows magic?" Bernadette asked, opening the refrigerator for milk to color the tea.

"No, no. Someone who desperately wants the same thing you want. I suspect Patrick is your best choice. He's obviously looking for more than a key here. Smart boy to have figured out this is where you are." Fiona sipped her tea. Then she put the cup down and walked to the door, opening it and looking up at the night sky. "The moon's not full for two weeks, but how close are we to All Hallows' Eve?"

"You mean Halloween?"

"Yes. Is it coming up?

"It's a week from Saturday."

"Ah, it's best to wait for that. All Hallows' Eve. At midnight."

PATRICK

TUESDAY, OCTOBER 20

Patrick got another e-mail from his mother, and this one was truly puzzling. It contained a list of things she needed him to get for her. One would be easy. One might be hard. One would be almost impossible.

He had to get them himself. It had to be secret.

He had reread the e-mail several times, to make sure he understood exactly what he had to do:

To: pmcbride@saltzmanms.edu
From: bmcbride@newsday.com
Subject: Important items
Date: 10/19 06:48:12 PM Daylight Saving Time

Patrick,
Believe it or not, getting out of here involves baking, and I'll need very specific ingredients. Think of it as the oddest scavenger hunt you've ever gone on.

Here's what I need: three sprigs of watercress, any kind. Ten gooseberries and ten thorns from a gooseberry bush. The watercress you can get at Pathmark. The gooseberries . . . Can you try a local nursery?

And this is the hard one, Patrick. I need an ember from a fire that was started on April 30—a May Eve fire. You will have to find someone here on Long Island who practices the tradition of keeping a fire started on May Eve going throughout the year. Grandma did, but even I didn't realize it until recently! There must be other immigrants who do it, too. You might call the Irish shop in Merrick (it's called Emerald Gifts and Goods) and ask the owner if she knows anyone. Can you say it's for a school report? (I know this is technically a lie, but just this once it's okay.) Once you get the ember, you must keep it alive—hot—so it can be used to start another fire. If it goes out, it's no good.

I need these things as soon as possible—by October 28 at the latest!

Also—you cannot tell anyone about this! And it's best, I think, if you can get these things without asking your dad for help. Write me back when you've gotten them, or if you are having trouble. We will have to arrange a place and time for you to drop these things off before the 28th. I love you. Me.

Patrick wondered what kind of kidnappers would demand baked goods as ransom. How in the world would these things help his mother get out of wherever she was? The ingredients reminded him, eerily, of the potions his grandmother often made. She had once closed a gash on his knee (he had fallen on the sharp end of a hoe) with something that looked like mashed weeds and smelled like garlic, spread on a cloth. It was amazing! The wound healed up almost instantly. He had tried to tell his father about it, but he sensed his father didn't believe him when he described how deep the gash had been before his grandmother's cure.

Patrick set to work immediately. He left for school Wednesday with money from his savings in his pocket. He rode his bike to school so he could go to the supermarket on his way home. He didn't buy the watercress, but he found out what it cost (it was cheap) and made sure they would have it when he got the other stuff.

After the grocery store, he went to a garden store on Conklin Street. He leaned his bike up against a split-rail fence, picked his way around mounds of pumpkins, and approached a man who was misting potted plants with a hose.

"Excuse me, sir. Do you work here?"

"Every day. How can I help you?"

"Do you sell gooseberry bushes?"

"Gooseberry bushes? No. Nobody sells gooseberry bushes."

Patrick's heart sank. "Nobody?"

"Well, nobody anymore. Not since the rust."

"The rust?"

"Rust. Blister rust. It's a fungus that thrives on the gooseberry bush. When it jumps to trees, it can kill 'em, especially pine. So the gooseberry's pretty much been eradicated around here."

Great, Patrick thought.

"Would a currant bush do you? It's very similar."

"I'm not sure."

"Is this a school project?"

"No. It's for my mom."

"She must be a vegetable gardener, right? Gardeners like

thorny bushes because they keep critters from eating their crops."

That jogged Patrick's brain. "Do you have a picture of what a gooseberry bush looks like?"

"I might. There's a big ol' book in the office with every plant in the world in it. Ask my wife. She's in there."

The office was lined with clay pots and straw baskets. A shiny aluminum garbage can held a bouquet of long-handled hoes and spades for sale. A woman at a desk was entering numbers on an adding machine, a ribbon of tape curling in big loops with every *ka-ching! ka-ching!* Patrick didn't want to disturb her, but after a moment she wrote some figures in a book and turned toward him. When he told her what he needed, she silently got the book from the shelf above her desk and placed it on the counter.

It was a thick book, like an encyclopedia of plants. There was a line drawing of the gooseberry, showing oval berries with faint white stripes. Patrick unzipped his backpack and got out a notebook. He drew a crude version of the plant on a sheet of lined paper.

"School project?" the lady asked.

"Right," Patrick answered, thanking her for the book and sealing his notebook back up in his bag. He had one more stop before home, and he needed to make it before it got dark.

He rode his bike to the entrance of the woods and cycled down the path to his grandmother's house, which he could just barely see through the trees. He leaned his bike next to an oak and walked between the trees up to her garden.

When the man at the nursery had said vegetable garden, Patrick remembered the pricks he often got weeding around his grandmother's lettuce. He got his notebook out and squatted down to the row of plants that bordered the plot where his grandmother had always planted her lettuce. He held the branch in his hand against the white paper. The berries looked similar and the sharp thorns stuck out at right angles, just like in his drawing. Well, Patrick thought, the gooseberry hasn't been completely eradicated after all.

That left just the impossible assignment. Thursday, Patrick got to social studies a few minutes early.

"Mr. Posnak, remember that paper I wrote on immigration?"

"Yes, Patrick, an excellent job."

"Well, I'd like to do some more research on Irish history."

"Really? That's commendable."

"Yeah, what I'm interested in is, um, Irish customs."

"Hmm. Which customs?"

"Well, like holding bonfires on May Eve."

"Oh, it sounds like you already know more about this than I do. Have you checked with the Hibernians?"

"Hibernians?"

"Yes. The Ancient Order of Hibernians. It's an Irish society."

"How do you spell that?"

Mr. Posnak spelled it out.

"Do they have a website? Like www.Hibernians.org?"

"A website? That I don't know. But Mrs. Fitzjames in the library would be able to help you find out. Have you approached her?"

"No, that's a good idea."

"Always happy to help students advance their knowledge

of history, Patrick." Other students had started to file into class. Patrick mumbled, "Thanks," and took his seat.

Patrick sat on the cold concrete step outside the seventh-grade wing and gobbled down his lunch. He was going to use his free period to go to the library. He should have thought of Mrs. Fitzjames himself. He had gotten to know her a little better because she was constantly teasing him about never having brought her a pass for the time he had been in the library to look at the back copies of the newspaper. She would threaten to turn him in, then pretend to relent so long as he carried some boxes for her or reshelved a few books. Mrs. Fitzjames had a lot of tricks to get students to help out.

In fact, Mrs. Fitzjames was the most fun librarian Patrick had ever come across. She ran the library like it was a sports team. When a student found something he was looking for, Mrs. Fitzjames would do a little victory jig like football players do in the end zone after they score, or she'd give out a high five. Every Friday, she wore a jersey with her name and the numbers 411 on the back.

"Is that 411, like you call to get telephone numbers?" Patrick asked her once.

"Yes! 'Information.' Get it? Not only that, but 411 is the Dewey decimal prefix for books about the alphabet!" she said. "Isn't that a miraculous little coincidence?" Clearly, Mrs. Fitzjames loved her job.

But Patrick's favorite thing about Mrs. Fitzjames was a photograph she had on her desk of herself and three boys, who Patrick thought were probably her sons. They were all hanging upside down from a set of monkey bars, even Mrs. Fitzjames. Patrick's mother would never hang upside down from the monkey bars, he thought, but then again, neither would I.

It was now easy to understand why Kevin had liked Mrs. Fitzjames as a catechism teacher. She could take the boring out of anything. Patrick also sensed—and right now this was key—that she was the kind of adult you could trust.

She was at her computer terminal, looking over the top of her reading glasses at the screen when Patrick came in.

"Hello, Mr. McBride. Got that pass you owe me?"

Patrick laughed. "No, and I don't have one to be here right now either."

"Oh?" she said, turning to look at him directly.

"It's my lunch period. I need some research help."

"What a scholar. Tell me."

"It's about Irish folklore."

"You've come to the right place. A library quarterbacked by a Fitzjames is the right place to begin your search for Irish folklore. But that's a big topic. What specifically are you interested in?"

How much could he say? It was supposed to be a secret. Was it okay to say what he was looking for so long as he didn't say why he needed it? "Well, I want to find out more about bonfires, about the custom of holding a bonfire on May Eve."

"Oooh. That's related to witchcraft. Fun stuff, Patrick. Let's check the Web."

She typed in some search words, then took a phone call while the computer did its searching.

She put her hand over the receiver. "Nearly three hundred sites on Irish folklore, Patrick. You want to start looking through them to see if any specialize in bonfires?"

"Sure," he mouthed quietly.

"Come around here. What's this for? A paper?"

"Well, no." Patrick could not lie to Mrs. Fitzjames, nor could he tell the truth. "It's something personal."

"Personal? Enough said. We librarians are big on privacy. Yes, I'm here," she said into the receiver. "I'm helping a student."

Patrick scrolled through the sites. Irish football. Step dancing. Irish music. Halfway through the second set of twenty, there was one called Local Ireland: New York. He dragged the cursor to it and clicked.

In the **Search** box, he typed in *folklore* and hit **Return**, but then his eye caught something along the right side of the screen.

CHAT ROOM.

His mother did not allow him to chat in anybody's online rooms, but maybe that was how he could find local people who might have what he needed: a roaring fire that had been going for six months.

He copied down the URL for the site while Mrs. Fitzjames was still talking. "Thank you," he whispered.

She cupped the phone. "Get what you needed?"

He put his hand high in the air, palm out. She laughed and gave him a high five.

"You're catching on, McBride."

BERNADETTE

TUESDAY, OCTOBER 20

Bernadette got to school early. She did not stop at her locker. She headed for the stairs. When she reached the top, she could see a teacher headed to the stairs at the other end of the hall, a coffee cup in her hand.

The computer lab was one of the few rooms that wasn't used as a homeroom. The lights hadn't been turned on yet, but when Bernadette turned the knob, the door slid open.

She crouched down behind Victoria's terminal and took out a plastic squeeze bottle of honey she had brought from home. She dribbled long strings over Q-W-E-R-T, then J-K-L and the semicolon, up and down the keyboard in a gooey zigzag and then across the top of the monitor and down its sides. She twisted the plastic lid closed and exchanged it in her coat pocket for a second jar, which held a small colony of ants. She had lured them into captivity by putting a glazed doughnut at the bottom of a jar and turning the jar on its side next to an anthill in the woods. She felt terrible sabotaging school property, but what choice had Victoria left her?

Then she left, closing the door behind her. She went downstairs, back outside, and walked slowly around the neighborhood. She put both jars in a garbage can at someone's curb. When she heard the second bell, she headed back to school.

"To the office," said a woman she knew to be the assistant principal, herding Bernadette and a few other stragglers. "Get your late passes."

Bernadette was sitting in first-period Language Arts when the intercom buzzed. The class had finished the unit on mystery and had moved on to mythology, a topic Bernadette thought was only useful to people who did crossword puzzles. A lot of stuff you learned in middle school *really* was irrelevant, she thought.

"Yes," Mrs. Christie called out.

"Detta Downey to the guidance office, please."

Mrs. Christie looked at Bernadette. "Should she bring her stuff?" she asked.

"No. Just herself."

Bernadette recognized Mrs. Piazza's voice. Did somebody see her leave the computer lab? She thought briefly about leaving school entirely, but she needed her backpack. Her Irish legends book was in it.

"Miss Downey. Long time no see."

"Is something wrong?"

"Yes. We do have a problem."

Bernadette suddenly remembered Mrs. Piazza having seen her at the ATM. She could feel sweat break out on her forehead. "Oh," was all she managed to say in response.

"Have a seat, Detta. You look like a frightened rabbit." She pulled a file out of a stack on her desk.

"Thanks."

"Here it is," Mrs. Piazza said, pulling a sheet from inside the folder. "It's this Social Security number you gave me. It comes back as belonging to somebody else. A forty-year-old guy named Morris Shinbaum, who lives in Bellport. You don't know Morris, do you?"

"No."

"I didn't think so. What is your Social Security number?"

"Um. Zero-nine-nine." She stopped herself. "That's all I remember. It begins with oh-nine-nine."

"That's the first thing I've known you *not* to know, Detta. Well, you'll have to bring me the actual card. Maybe you just transposed a digit, but now I've got to make a copy of it to satisfy them."

"Okay. Can I go back to class?"

"Yes, be gone."

Bernadette knew she wasn't going to be able to produce the card, but at the moment she was simply relieved that she hadn't been discovered as the saboteur of the computer.

"And Detta?"

"Yes?"

"I need it yesterday."

Bernadette walked down the hall, away from the guidance office, before taking a huge breath. She wouldn't be able to face Mrs. Piazza again without the card, that was for sure. This was her last day as a seventh grader.

In gym, the class was doing a unit on gymnastics. Ally had been trying to teach Bernadette how to do something called a glide kip, which was a simple mount, on the uneven parallel bars. It took incredible strength in the stomach muscles, so Ally had Bernadette doing sit-ups every day to tone her abdominals. Bernadette had had to admit to herself this bit of vanity: She loved having a flat stomach again.

"Jump onto the bar and swing out, all the way," Ally said. "Pretend you're trying to touch the far wall with your toes. Total extension."

Bernadette concentrated. There were about six things Ally insisted you had to do to complete this one move. She wondered how gymnasts could concentrate on so many things at once, but then she thought mothers were always concentrating on several things at once, too. Your mind adjusts. She jumped to the low bar, swinging her legs out in a V before bringing them together. Then she had to fold herself in half, the top of her feet lightly tapping the low bar, before her arms pushed her torso upright. All this happened in about five seconds.

"That's it!" Ally cried. "That was fabulous. Good form and everything!"

Bernadette beamed.

"Tomorrow we can build on this and teach you some basic wraparounds," Ally said.

"Or maybe I'll just relish my mastery of the glide kip for a while," Bernadette said.

Ally laughed. "I have to keep my ambition in check, right?"

"No, *you* don't," Bernadette said. "But I do."

At lunch, Annmarie was giving a play-by-play of the romance between a girl she sat next to in math class and a boy who was sitting at the next table.

"It's their three-week tomorrow," she whispered. "Only he doesn't even talk to her at school. She says the only time he'll talk to her is on the telephone."

"Why?" Judy asked.

"Who knows? But when he's with his friends, he pretends she doesn't exist."

"I'd break up with him," Donna said.

"She's madly in love! She has his name written in the margins of every page in her notebook."

Bernadette looked around at the faces of Donna, Annmarie, and Judy. Beautiful faces. She hoped she would see them again. She hoped she would come to this school as Patrick's mother to watch them in a play, or as part of the chorus. She thought how happy she would be if, one day, Patrick came home and told her, "I have asked a girl to go to the prom and her name is Donna. You'll like her." Would Donna be Patrick's type? Did Patrick *have* a type? She didn't know. What if it turned out Victoria Cavendish was Patrick's type?

Don't go there, she told herself.

She reluctantly turned in her flute, telling the band director her homework was getting burdensome, so she was going to have to cut back on her activities. "I never mastered it," she said.

"But you were trying," he said. "I could tell. You should try something else before you give up music entirely. That's always a mistake."

"You're right," she told him. "I'll think about it."

When she got to computer class that afternoon, Victoria was at a terminal in the last row, looking very unhappy. Victoria's computer was gone, keyboard, hard drive, monitor, and all. Not a word was said about it.

After she took her seat, Patrick came in. When he reached his desk, he plopped his backpack on the ground and turned toward her.

"Hey, thanks for getting Victoria off my case yesterday," he said as the rest of the class was filing in.

Bernadette was momentarily rendered speechless. "You're welcome," she managed.

"I'm Patrick," he said.

"Detta," she said, her eyes flashing toward the front of the classroom, hoping Ms. Dobbs would start and rescue her from this conversation. She was unbelievably nervous that Patrick would figure out who she was.

"I see we've gotten rid of her today," he said, nodding toward Victoria's vacant space.

"Yeah—and her computer, too," Bernadette replied, careful not to reveal more than she ought to.

"Well, thanks again. You didn't go to Woodward Parkway Elementary, did you? You look so familiar."

"No, I just moved here this year," she said.

"Where do you live?" he asked, and then the class did start. Patrick whispered, "Talk to you later," and faced front.

Bernadette then watched him read the e-mail she had sent him the night before, copy out the list, and delete the message. She wondered how he would find the things she needed when she wouldn't even know how to get two of them herself.

What came to mind, curiously, was what Ally had said to her that first day they teamed up in gym class, and Ally had taught Bernadette how to turn herself upside down. "You just have to trust me. And yourself." She wound up trusting Ally a lot. She was capable and confident. Why was it easier to feel that way about Ally than about her own child? Bernadette had asked Patrick to do some weird things, but he was capable and confident, too, she recognized, supremely so. Now she had to trust that he could get these things she desperately needed and still land okay. Upside down, maybe. Dizzy, maybe. But okay.

Since the day the police came, Bernadette had gotten increasingly nervous about the neighbors on William Street. It was amazing that they had taken no notice of her, but she herself rarely saw anyone home during the day. One time she thought she saw a curtain fall in the Cunninghams' old house as she passed by.

Just to be on the safe side, she had established a practice of going to the library until closing time, then walking the long way home, past her house on Jackson Avenue, through the woods behind the high school, and into her mother's yard from the back, after it was dark.

She had left all her textbooks in her locker, so her backpack was light. She could use more reading material, but she wondered if it was wise to use the library card again. She made up her mind that if the clerk was unfamiliar, she would risk it.

But when she got to the library, there was a sheriff's-department cruiser parked at the curb. This couldn't be about her, could it? Libraries didn't keep track of things like banks did, did they?

But she couldn't take a chance. She looked through the rectangle of glass into the building, and she could see two officers, leaning against the checkout counter, talking to two of the ladies who worked there. Bernadette pulled her hat down farther on her head and scrammed.

PATRICK

The third game of the World Series was beginning on the living-room television. Normally, no force in the world could have separated Patrick from the TV during the series. But Patrick had not been able to get into the chat room from his computer at school and had not had an opportunity to use his parents' computer, upstairs. This was his moment, because it would take the most powerful force in the *universe* to separate his father and brothers from the TV. Even if his mother rang the doorbell now, they might not answer it.

"Be right back," he said, as Sheryl Crow finished singing the National Anthem.

Patrick typed in the URL for the Local Ireland site. It appeared on his screen, and he dragged the mouse to the chat-room icon.

Screen name? it asked him.

He typed in: Mookie. The TV broadcasters had just been talking about Mookie Wilson, hero of the last World Series the Mets played in. Patrick's father had wanted to name him

Mookie, because Patrick had arrived the year after that World Series, but his mother refused.

Been here before? the screen read. **If not, please register.**

There were a bunch of rules, which Patrick skimmed, quickly clicking on the button that said he had read and agreed to abide by them. He watched as "Mookie" popped into the chat room. There were seven other people on-line: Siobhan, Shenanigans, Susannah, Loretta, Paddy, Moira J., and Big John.

His presence was acknowledged immediately:

Shenanigans: Welcome to our thatched roof cottage, Mookie! How come you're not at the game? Har, Har, Har.
Mookie: Busy. Does anyone know anyone who holds a bonfire on April 30? A May Eve bonfire?
Loretta: Oh, Mookie, that's an ancient custom. Not the same crowd as sits in chat rooms, thatched roof or no.

Arrrrgh, Patrick thought. That was surely true.

Susannah: Have you tried the Hibernians?
Mookie: Who are these Hibernians? How do you get in touch with them?
Big_John: I don't know about the Hibernians, but my mother keeps the practice, though I've tried to get her to give it up. In fact, it's against the law, because she does it in the back-yard. But she insists a fire started with an ember from the bonfire keeps evil at bay, so I make sure the fire doesn't get out of control.
Mookie: Does she have a fire going now?

Big_John: Oh, yeah. She keeps the fire going all year, even through the hottest days of August. Tends it like a baby. What do you need to know about it?

Patrick nearly cried out in joy. He started to type in that he was writing a report for school, but stopped his fingers before they hit the **Enter** button and deleted that. He thought he remembered that one of the rules said you had to be eighteen to be in the chat room.

Mookie: I'm doing research.

Shenanigans: An intellectual in the cottage, folks. Try yer best to sound intelligent, though it'll be hard for the rest of ye. Queen's English only.

Big_John: Well, she's not big on computers. Do you have some questions? I could relay them.

Mookie: Can you ask her if she'd be interviewed?

Big_John: She's not big on the telephone, either.

Mookie: How about in person?

Moira_J.: You wouldn't be a scammer now, Mookie, would you? There's none of that permitted in our digicottage.

Mookie: No. I'm honest.

Shenanigans: An honest intellectual. Another first in the thatched cottage.

Big_John: Hang on, Mookie. I'll ask her. Check back with me after the bottom of the first. I've got to check the score, too.

Patrick went downstairs.

"You're missing the game," Kevin said.

"Homework."

"What kind of cruel teacher would assign homework during the World Series?" Kevin asked. "Furthermore, what kind of sick puppy would *do* it?"

"That's enough, Kevin," their father said.

"What's the score?"

"Zero to zero," Neil said.

Patrick watched until the Mets made the third out. "Call me if they get a rally going," he said. Upstairs, he signed back on and reentered the chat room.

Mookie: You there, Big John?
Big_John: She'll do it, so long as I'm there. She's interested in keeping the old customs alive. Where are you?
Mookie: Farmingdale. Where are you?
Big_John: Not too far. We're in Queens. Woodside. You know it?

Queens? Patrick thought. Not too far? Not too far, if you drive a car.

Mookie: How would I get there from the train?
Big_John: The LIRR?
Mookie: Right.
Big_John: Easy. We live two blocks from the station.

Okay, there's a break, Patrick thought.

Mookie: How do I get there? And when?
Big_John: You got an e-mail address, Mookie? I'll send you directions. I don't want Shenanigans to know where I live. He's a moocher.

Shenanigans: Now, you're giving the professor the wrong impression of me, Big J.

Big_John: What's wrong about it?

Shenanigans: I only mooch from friends, not the general population, and only in pubs, not in private homes.

Mookie: How soon can we do this?

Big_John: Well, I gotta work tomorrow and Monday, and I've got tickets to Saturday and Sunday's games, but I got a Kelly Day Tuesday. How about Tuesday, around noon?

Mookie: Tuesday noon is good. What's a Kelly Day?

Big_John: It's a day off. A day off for a firefighter.

A firefighter, Patrick thought. Whose mother keeps a fire going all year long. Why did this sound problematic if what you intended was to leave the house with a burning ember and travel thirty miles by train with it? He tapped in his e-mail address. If Big John figured out it was a middle school, Patrick would have to lie and say he was a teacher.

Would they simply give him an ember? What could he say to get them to agree to that? Would a firefighter let him leave the house with a live ember? Once the firefighter saw he was not a professor or a researcher writing a book, but a kid?

No. The answer was definitely no.

He would have to steal the ember.

And he would have to do something else.

He would have to get Kevin to help.

BERNADETTE

Bernadette felt like a prisoner, trapped in the house, but it turned out to be a good thing. Her mother showed her how to make soda bread—something Bernadette never made anymore, because she couldn't get it to come out as good as her mother's.

"The buttermilk is the key to a fine bread," her mother told her, pouring the milk directly into a lump of flour on the counter. "I don't know how much you use. I've never measured it. Just keep adding until the bread feels barely sticky."

"How come you never use a bowl to do this?"

"You can't properly knead a bread in a bowl. It must be a flat surface."

In the evenings they sat by the fire, and Bernadette played reporter, asking her mother questions about the various herbs she grew in her garden and their uses, about fairies, about her childhood.

She finally summoned the nerve to ask: "Mom, are you a witch?"

"Am I a witch? Are you mad?"

"Well, I don't understand—"

"That word has a lot of luggage."

"Baggage, you mean." Bernadette laughed.

"Baggage, right. No, I'm not a witch. I'm a close observer of the way the world works. Witches are, too, but they use what they learn to make mischief. I use what I know to keep the little people in line, just as my grandmother did."

"Your grandmother taught you all this?"

"She taught me how to handle fairies—how to keep them in line. She taught me too well, in fact. They followed me here, all the way across the Atlantic, and I have never been able to shake them."

By Monday, Bernadette felt she had to do something to cover her absence at school. Over the weekend, thinking about Patrick, wondering what he was up to, she remembered that when her kids were out of school, she always got an automated call, reporting their absence. She had made up the phone number she put on her enrollment forms. Where were those calls going? She had visions of Mrs. Piazza at the front door with a bullhorn and a battering ram if she didn't come to school for a few days without any explanation. She would have to call the school, but she was down to her last twenty cents, not even enough to use a pay phone.

Her mother was eating breakfast in the kitchen when Bernadette came down the stairs Monday morning in her pajamas.

"Have you quit school?"

"I can't go anymore," Bernadette said, taking a teacup out of the cupboard. "They're figuring out I don't belong there."

"What a shame. You had become such a scholar."

"Mom, I have to call them and make up some excuse, otherwise the truant officer might come knocking on the door. Do you have a few coins?"

"Did you check the coffee can?"

"Oh—the coffee can. Is there still money in there?" Bernadette poured boiling water into the cup. She had forgotten that her mother always kept the household money in an old Maxwell House can in the pantry.

"Yes, there's plenty there. Unless the fairies got it."

"What!" Bernadette sputtered, nearly dropping the hot kettle. "Fairies steal money? I thought fairies slept in flowers and drank dew! You never told me they stole money."

"Fairies steal everything, Bernadette. Anything of value."

"So why don't they take it out of the coffee can?"

"Because fairies will not go near anything metal. Bernadette—I told you all this as a girl."

"You did? I only remembered the Tinker Bell parts. No, wait. Is that why you always insisted I keep my allowance in that cookie tin?"

"Precisely."

Bernadette shook her head. "I still have that tin. Neil has his rock collection in it now." She crossed to the pantry and stood on a stepstool to reach the coffee can on the top shelf. It was surprisingly heavy. She pried off its plastic lid. There was a thick coil of bills, sitting on a mountain of coins. Bernadette pulled out the wad of money and spread the bills in a fan. It was mostly hundred-dollar bills—thousands of dollars—too much to count at a glance.

"Mother, what on earth are you doing with all this money?"

"Oh, I stopped bothering with the bank long ago. It's yours. Same as the rest of what's here."

"I just need a quarter," Bernadette said, but as she fished to retrieve a whole handful of change, an idea quickly formed, and she giggled.

"What's funny?" her mother asked.

"I just thought of a good cause for this windfall." She could already see the plaque: THE FIONA DOWNEY MEMORIAL COMPUTER LAB.

Bernadette dressed quickly, left the house through the kitchen door, and walked to the shopping center near Fiona's house. The sun was shining, but the air had a sharp, cold edge. The newsstand there had a pay phone, one of those old-fashioned kind inside a booth, with a hinged door. She dug into the pocket of her white hip-huggers—no easy task, that—for thirty-five cents, then pushed the door closed. She dialed the number for the school.

"Paul A. Saltzman Middle School, how may I help you?"

"Attendance, please."

There was a pause while the call was transferred.

"This is Carolyn."

"Hello, my name is Detta Downey. I was absent from school three days last week." Bernadette paused to fake a cough, barely turning her mouth away from the receiver.

"Downey. Yes, I left your parents a message Friday. Is this

the correct number for you?" She read the made-up phone number Bernadette had given Mrs. Piazza.

"Yes, they got it. That's why I'm calling." Bernadette was thankful for answering machines, and working mothers. Whoever had gotten that message must have ignored it. "I won't be bringing in a note today, because I have the chicken pox. The doctor says I'll be out for the week."

"Another week?"

"It's a severe case."

"Well, someone will have to get your work for you. Can I speak to your mother? I can take you off the truant list so she won't get the recorded message every day."

"She went to the pharmacy for calamine lotion," Bernadette said. "The itching is driving me nuts."

"Oh, poor dear. Okay, I'll note the record and remove you from the list, but have her either give me a call or stop by with a note."

"Okay."

"Feel better."

"Thanks."

On her way out, Bernadette lingered to look at the headlines. The big draws at the newsstand were probably cigarettes and lottery tickets, but she had always come to buy the *Irish Echo* for her mother, or the Sunday *Times* for herself. The store was owned by a couple, who were always there, working alongside each other. They had been middle-aged when Bernadette first noticed them. Their hair had gone white now. The wife ran the register. The husband patrolled the aisles. He was standing behind Bernadette now, slicing bands off stacks of new magazines.

"You see this?" the wife said, the newspaper open on the

counter before her. "That missing woman? Now the cops say somebody's been using her computer."

"Oh yeah?" he said. "How do they know that?"

Bernadette picked up a copy of *Newsday* and pretended to read the back page. Her heart started thumping, fast.

"Well, she works for the newspaper and apparently it was the newspaper's computer," the wife said. "It says they 'detected use in her company e-mail account,' whatever that means, 'but declined to give further details.' It doesn't say. Jeez, you think the newspaper would have the scoop on its own story."

"See? That's why I don't trust the Internet and all that jazz," the husband said. "Big Brother can trace everything. These people using credit cards in the information supermarket? They're asking for trouble. Missy, shouldn't you be in school by now?"

"Yes, sorry," Bernadette said. He had caught her listening to their conversation. She walked to the counter with the newspaper.

"Fifty cents, dear," the wife said. Bernadette put the money on the counter.

Bernadette stuffed the paper under her arm and started walking.

She read the whole story at home, and she could tell from the managing editor's quotes that he was deliberately leaving out the details. The newspaper wouldn't be keen on giving the police access to *anything* on their computers, for any reason. But maybe the technology guys could read her e-mails and figured out she was not in the hands of criminals. That would make the editors doubly reluctant to break a precedent and give the police access to newsroom data.

Either way, the lady at the newsstand was right. The story was annoyingly vague on what this development meant to police, Bernadette's family, or her status as a suspiciously missing person.

But one thing was sure. She couldn't use her computer anymore. Not unless she wanted to be revealed as a twelve-year-old. What if Patrick couldn't get the stuff she needed for the soul cakes? What if—and here was a distinct possibility as far as Bernadette was concerned—what if the soul cake cure didn't work? Could she just go show up at home and say, *"It's me!"*

"Bad idea," her mother said, when Bernadette asked her about it.

"Why?"

"You're under the power of fairies. You don't want to introduce that into your family. You want out. Fairies are not benevolent creatures."

But how would Bernadette get in touch with Patrick now?

PATRICK

TUESDAY, OCTOBER 27

Patrick and Kevin agreed to leave for school as usual. Patrick would meet Duffy and Kyle at the corner and pretend to be sick. He would head toward home and keep walking. Kevin would drop Neil off at his classroom and quickly leave the building.

"We'll meet at the train station at nine," Patrick reminded him.

"Aye, aye, Captain."

"Kevin, don't kid around. This is serious."

"It has to be serious if Mr. Goody Two-Shoes is cutting school and encouraging *me* to cut school. Why can't you tell me what it is?"

"Just meet me there at nine."

"Nine A.M. Eastern, eight Central. I'll be there."

Patrick had put oven mitts, tongs, and a ceramic dish with a lid in his backpack. The dish was stamped OVENPROOF on the bottom. He had the morning newspaper and a baggie full of dried leaves.

The day before, after school, he had gone to Pathmark and bought the watercress. Then he picked ten thorns and ten berries from the bush in his grandmother's garden. He had the key to her house in his pocket, but he didn't have time to try it in the front door because Mrs. Compton, whom Kevin had renamed Mrs. Incompetent, had a bad toothache and had to go to the dentist at four. Patrick had promised his father he would be home by the time she had to leave. He wondered if he'd get paid a portion of her salary. Ha-ha, he thought.

His mother's deadline was one day away. If, today, everything went according to plan, he would make it. The only problem was he didn't *have* a plan. Stealing an ember from a fireplace in a home you've never been in before is tough to plan.

The curious thing was, since the e-mail a week ago, he had not heard from his mother. He had sent back a message saying he got the list, then a message saying he thought he would be able to get all three things by Tuesday afternoon, but she hadn't responded. This was worrisome.

Patrick was waiting on the platform when he saw Kevin coming up the escalator.

"Which way we going, Doc?" Kevin asked.

"Westbound. And we have some time to kill. We don't need to be where we're going until noon."

"When are you going to tell me what we're doing?"

"I'm not going to tell you *why* we're doing it, so don't bug me, but I will tell you what you need to do. We're going to this old lady's house, Mrs. Crone. Her son's going to be there, too."

"Here comes the train," Kevin said, nodding down the tracks.

"She is going to tell us about bonfires," Patrick said, raising his voice to be heard over the noise of the train. "WHILE I DISTRACT HER, YOU ARE GOING TO TAKE A HOT EMBER FROM HER FIREPLACE AND GET OUT OF THERE WITH IT."

"ARE YOU OUT OF YOUR MIND?" Kevin shouted as the train rumbled into the station.

"AND YOU'VE GOT TO TAKE A PIECE BIG ENOUGH TO STAY HOT UNTIL WE CAN GET IT HOME. SOMETHING THAT WILL FIT IN THIS BAKING DISH I HAVE IN HERE." Patrick gestured at the backpack as the train pulled to a stop. "I have oven mitts and tongs, too," he said, almost in a whisper. "We have to get the ember home while it's still hot enough to use to start another fire."

"Let me look in your ears. Yep. Just what I thought. NOTHING in there."

"Get on the train."

"Patrick, really, what are we doing?"

"Shut UP. Pick a seat."

The train ride took only a half hour, so Patrick and Kevin went to a coffee shop in Woodside and had breakfast again.

"You paying for this?" Kevin asked.

"Yes."

"It's possible this is my last meal using my hands, so can I get dessert, too?" Kevin asked.

"What are you talking about?"

"Well after handling hot embers, who knows what shape my poor mitts will be in. . . ."

"Get dessert."

They found Big John's house without any trouble. It was 10:45 A.M.

"Let's wait till eleven," Patrick said. "It's okay if we're a little early."

"Yeah, the element of surprise is always important when you're robbing a log that's on fire."

"You know what to do?"

"Give me the backpack." Kevin took out the tongs and the oven mitts and put them in his coat pocket. "Is this Mom's rice-pudding dish? She's gonna kill you."

"As soon as you can, put the ember in it. If you have to, use the stuff in the bags or strips of newspaper to keep the ember hot, but try not to create too much heat, because we have to get back on the train with this."

"How much money do you have?"

"Enough. Why?"

"Enough for *bail*?"

Patrick rezipped the backpack and gently inched it over his shoulders. "Once you get the ember, start walking toward the train station and I'll catch up with you. Ready?"

"Is this some sort of dare? Did McDuff bet you that you couldn't get me to do this?"

"This has nothing to do with Duffy or Kyle. This is the most important thing you've ever done in your lousy life."

"Well, then, Captain," Kevin said, tugging the collar of his jacket straight, "I'm ready."

———

Mrs. Crone lived in a narrow three-story brownstone. There were steep steps climbing up to her front door, a pot with a wilted geranium in it, and a green-and-gold hand-painted sign hanging from a nail on the door that read, DIA GO LEAGA AN RATH ORT.

"Is this lady Spanish?" Kevin asked.

"That's not Spanish, that's Gaelic."

"How do you know?"

"I'm guessing. Don't take that hat off, skinhead. You might scare her," Patrick said as he rang the bell. "And don't *say* anything."

The door opened a crack. An impossibly small woman stood before them, both hands leaning on a craggy walking stick.

"I'm not buying any cookies this year," peering at them through the slit of the open door, the swag of the safety chain level with her nose.

"No, ma'am, Mrs. Crone? I'm Patrick McBride. Your son told me you could tell me about bonfires."

"My eyes are going, but you look awfully young to be a professor."

"I'm a student. Doing research."

"And who's your assistant?"

"That's my brother."

"Well, come in. You don't look like hoodlums, and you'll be disappointed if you are. The robbers have already cleaned me out."

The house was dark and every surface appeared to be covered with a doily of intricate ivory lace. Mrs. Crone led them into a parlor. There was a framed photograph of the pope—not the current one, Patrick thought, but some previous pope—on the mantel. Right beneath it in the grate, he saw a crackling fire.

"Johnny's here, but he's sacked out. He had a four-alarm at two A.M. in Brighton Beach, just as he was to go off duty," she said, plopping herself down into a wingback chair. "He told me you're interested in the May Eve rituals?"

"Yes, in the bonfires, specifically," Patrick said, his eyes fixed on the fireplace. "Did you start this fire with an ember from a May Eve bonfire?"

"Yes, I did. A small bonfire, because Johnny's very particular about me not setting the neighborhood ablaze."

"Do you make the bonfire right here?" Patrick asked.

"Well, not here. In the yard, of course."

"In the yard, that's what I meant. Could you show me where, specifically?"

"Well, there's nothing to see, is there? There's no fire there now."

"Yes, but it might help me get a sense of how it works if I saw where you built it."

"It wouldn't help you at all. It's just a plain square of grass."

"Do you build it in a pit?" This was Kevin. Patrick flashed him an angry look.

"Heavens, no. Johnny moves the birdbath. He grouses the whole time because it's heavy as a lorry. We build the fire inside the stone circle that surrounds the bath."

"Oh, a stone circle!" Patrick said. "Is there some reason for the circle? Like crop circles?"

"Crop circles? What in heaven's name are you talking about? It's just a bit of landscaping. Johnny insists we build the fire inside the stones to contain it a bit. Well, you are a persistent pair. Come, I'll show you the famous birdbath. Maybe there'll even be a bird there." As Mrs. Crone pushed out of the chair, Patrick stole a glance at Kevin, who was winking like he had something in his eye and giving him a thumbs-up sign.

Patrick followed Mrs. Crone through a tiny kitchen to a narrow hallway at the back of the house. She opened a door, stepping out onto a concrete step. "See the birdbath there? Fascinating, isn't it?" There were two gray pigeons perched on it. Both turned and looked directly at them.

Patrick was trying to think up a question he could ask to prolong the view of the birdbath when he heard a *pssst* behind him. Kevin was wearing the oven mitts and tossing a log from hand to hand.

"Nasty pigeons. They hog the bath and scare away the songbirds," Mrs. Crone complained.

"Is this enough?" Kevin whispered.

"Yes, I'm sure that's enough," Mrs. Crone said. "As I told you, there's nothing to see." She moved to shut the door.

"Go!" Patrick mouthed back to him.

Mrs. Crone quaked with a shiver. "Chilly out there. I'll put the kettle on."

Patrick overcame his strong urge to be polite. "Well, ma'am, thank you for the information. This will help me when I write my report," Patrick said.

"But I haven't even begun!"

"Yes, but it's a very short report. This was plenty. Thank you again," Patrick said, backing away, toward the front door. It was ajar, and when he turned he could see Kevin outside, hopping up and down on the sidewalk, still tossing the log from hand to hand.

"Nice to meet you," he yelled. He took the entire front steps in one jump. He decided it was a lucky break that Mrs. Crone was hobbled and couldn't chase him.

"Yow! This thing is hot," Kevin said.

"It's on fire, you idiot! Put it in the pot."

"The pot is in the backpack, *idiot,*" Kevin said.

"Sorry." Patrick shrugged the backpack off, quickly unzipped it, and removed the dish. "Is she looking at us?"

"I don't think so. She's probably waking the fireman."

At the station, Patrick held the pot in his lap, until it got too warm. Then he put it down, beneath the bench, on the station platform.

"We're going to have to keep this hidden on the train," Patrick said.

"Duh."

"We'll have to keep it under the seat, with the lid off a little so it can breathe."

"Wait until I tell my friends what I did the first time I cut school. Went to an old lady's house, stole a log from her fireplace, and then hid it on the train. Is this what they consider fun in middle school?"

An eastbound train pulled into the station. "Look for the emptiest car," Patrick said.

Patrick had bought round-trip tickets, and the conductor would be around to punch them for sure. Patrick kept checking on the log while Kevin acted as lookout. They passed half a dozen stops without anyone official coming through their car. Patrick hoped that maybe since it wasn't rush hour, no one would come by.

The train pulled into Wantagh. Patrick saw a woman in a

railroad uniform step onto the platform from the car just ahead of the one he and Kevin were in. Two people stopped to talk to her, then all three of them got on the train, one car ahead. The doors closed and the train pulled away.

"There's smoke," Kevin said, pointing beneath the seat.

"Darn it, I fed it too much. And here comes the conductor."

"Can't we just say it's a casserole we're bringing to a sick friend?"

"A casserole doesn't smoke!"

"It's a special smoking casserole. Here, give it to me. Gimme the mitts, too."

Kevin walked off with the dish in front of him as the conductor entered the car. There was a small bathroom at the far end of the car. Patrick watched Kevin open the door and go inside. When he turned around, it was clear the conductor had been watching him, too.

"Tickets, please."

"These are for both of us," Patrick said, handing her the tickets. "He had, um, an emergency."

"You aren't smoking in here, are you? This is a no-smoking train."

"We don't smoke."

"Smells funny in here. Shouldn't you be in school?"

"We're home-schooled."

"Home-schooled. That's a new one." She handed the tickets back to Patrick. "No mischief, buddy. You've got two more stops."

"Thank you."

She opened the end doors to pass to the next car. The train was pulling into a station. As it slowed, Patrick could read the sign. SEAFORD, it said. He was just about to go knock on the bathroom door to tell Kevin the coast was clear when he heard a piercing wail, coming from the bathroom. The door flew open.

"Smoke detector," Kevin said, running to the exit with the dish in his hands. "We're busted."

They jumped off the train the moment the doors opened and fled to the stairs.

"Here, take this thing," Kevin screamed. "My hands are about to be grilled."

Patrick pulled the sleeves of his coat over his hands and took the dish. He trotted, awkwardly, holding the lid to the baking dish a little askew so the ember would get air. After he and Kevin crossed the street, they slowed the pace but kept walking, until they came to a little public green with a gazebo.

"Gimme the mitts," Patrick said. "We gotta check the ember."

The log was still hot. Patrick fed it some newspaper strips.

"Now what, Einstein?" Kevin asked. "Do you have disguises for us so we can get back on the next train?"

"We'll get a cab."

"A cab! That'll cost a mint. Just how much money do you have for this project?"

"This is the last of my birthday money."

"I thought you were buying a bigger amp."

"I thought so, too."

The cabdriver asked no questions about the baking dish and Patrick gave him all the money he had, which was probably not nearly as big a tip as he deserved.

There were two flashing blinks on the answering machine. Patrick listened to the messages. One from his school; one from Kevin's. Then he erased them.

"I need you to baby-sit," Patrick said. Kevin had already settled in front of the couch.

"We got an hour until Neil is out of school!"

"Not Neil. This ember. Keep it alive. Feed it strips of the newspaper and the leaves. Whatever you remember from Boy Scouts on how to tend a fire. Your life depends on it."

"Where are you going?"

Patrick opened the front door to go, but then he turned around again. "Kevin, thanks for helping me today. You were great."

"You mean you think I have a future in burning-log theft? Because I hear that field is wide open."

Patrick shook his head. "Don't let that fire die. I'll be right back."

Patrick knew the only doors to his school that were always unlocked from the outside were the front doors, but he couldn't chance being stopped at the office. Instead, he went around to the back, to the gym. He crossed his fingers as he pulled on the door and it opened. There was a class in the gym, but the teacher paid no attention to him.

He headed straight for the computer lab. Class had already started.

"Sorry I'm late, Ms. Dobbs," he said.

"Do you have a pass?" she asked.

Patrick went up to her desk and whispered: "No. I was sick in the bathroom."

"Don't you want to go home?"

"Yes, maybe I do. But I'll send my dad an e-mail at work to let him know. I tried calling him, but he was with a patient. He checks his e-mail frequently, though."

"Good idea," Ms. Dobbs said. She went back to her paperback novel.

Patrick didn't even look at Duffy, though he could feel his eyes on him. He went to his desk, hit the button on the monitor, and looked straight ahead at the screen. He clicked on his mailbox. **Messages waiting: 0**, it read.

He moved the mouse to the toolbar and clicked on **Write Mail**.

To: bmcbride@newsday.com
From: pmcbride@saltzmanms.edu
Subject: Urgent
Date: 10/27 1:44:24 PM Eastern Standard Time

Mom, I got the stuff. Where do we meet?

BERNADETTE

Bernadette had spent the entire day watching trains. The clocks had been turned back over the weekend, so by five o'clock, an inky darkness had settled over the station, punctuated by the overhead lights on the platform. She was cold, and though she had brought food in her coat pocket, it was gone and she was getting hungry, too. She longed for . . . a cup of coffee. She desperately wanted to be forty years old and drinking coffee again. She couldn't believe she had forgotten how miserable it was to be twelve, with no money and no transportation. She had even found herself craving a little housework, since vacuuming always had the effect of clearing her mind.

Yesterday she had perched in a tree across from the middle school watching for Patrick. She had followed him to Pathmark, her mother's house, then home. Then this morning, she had crouched behind a ficus hedge at the end of Jackson Avenue when Patrick reached Duffy and Kyle at the corner. He had said something to them, his hand on his stomach, then turned around and headed home. She had known immediately this was not genuine illness. She *was* his mother, after all.

She walked a block behind him, all the way to the train station. When he took the escalator to the platform, she took the stairs at the opposite end. She hid herself behind a *Wall Street Journal* someone had left on a bench, looking over the top of its pages, pretending to read a story on orange-juice futures. She nearly fell off the bench when she saw Kevin jump from the third step of the escalator onto the platform.

What had Patrick told Kevin? Could this hurt her chances of getting home?

No, she decided. Now she had two people pulling her out. That couldn't hurt. So long as Kevin behaved. She began to fret again. Maybe Patrick hadn't told him everything. Where were they going? Maybe the lady at the gift shop in Merrick had been able to help them.

As the afternoon wore on, the trains came faster and dislodged hordes of people. Bernadette could no longer see all of them or watch every exit, so she couldn't be sure she hadn't missed Patrick and Kevin. Could they still be wherever it was they went? What had they told their father? Had she sent them on a dangerous errand?

Fret, worry, fret, worry, fret. She was nearly sick. She was running out of ideas. She was running out of time. Finally, she gave up waiting.

She walked home, the long way, down Jackson Avenue. Gerard's car wasn't there, but the lights were on in her house. *Somebody* was home. She crossed the street. She slowed down as she passed in front of the house, looking intently through the picture window into the living room.

She saw Kevin's head.

And she saw something else. A ribbon of smoke escaping from the chimney. There was a fire in the fireplace.

They must have done it! she thought. She was jumping up and down on the sidewalk, her fists pumping the air. Until she realized how strange that would appear. Then she ran. She ran all the way to her mother's house.

Wednesday morning, Bernadette was crouched behind the hedge again. She saw Patrick coming up the street. Duffy and Kyle were on the corner, taking turns pushing each other into a bush. Could that be fun? she wondered.

"*Psssst,* Patrick," she called out. He glanced her way, looked at the Baxters, and crossed the street.

"I'm here to get the stuff your mother needs."

"You're the girl in my computer class. Detta, right?"

"Right. Can you go home and get it now?"

"How do you know my mother?"

"I'm helping her." Would he buy this? She considered begging.

"How can I be sure?"

"How else would I know you have stuff your mother needs?"

Patrick looked unconvinced. Bernadette tried another tack. "I know something else: Your father wanted to name you Mookie."

"Every kid my age was almost named Mookie, even some

of the girls," he said. "Did you move here this year or did you go to Saltzman last year, too, because I am *sure* I have met you before."

"We have met before."

"Where?"

"In a previous life. I can prove it." Bernadette put her fingers to her temples and closed her eyes. "You have a key in your pocket. A key other than the key to your own house."

Patrick looked puzzled. "Yeah, I do. How did you know that?"

Bernadette was glad she knew her son well enough to know he wouldn't hand off his hard-won collection to just anyone. Before heading out that morning, she used the extra key from the bottom of the Belleek vase to take the padlock off the shed. She reached into the pocket of her coat and produced it, a brass square with a silver metal loop. "It fits this lock. Try it."

Patrick took the lock. He fit the key into the hole on the bottom of the brass square and turned it. The loop twisted free.

"I thought this was the key to my grandmother's house. Where did you get this lock?"

"Your mother gave it to me. She told me to say that it was the key to her heart, then she told me *not* to say that because you would blush like a tomato if I did."

Patrick laughed. "Wait here," he said. He crossed to the corner and pulled Duffy out of the bush, which was getting the worst of the shoving match. Patrick said something to Kyle, who faked a punch at Patrick's stomach, then straightened his Mets cap and walked off, in the direction of school.

Duffy stood there talking to Patrick for another moment, then ran to catch up to his brother.

Bernadette watched Patrick walk home. He was back a few minutes later, a small paper shopping bag swinging from his arm, his two hands, gloved in the oven mitts, holding a casserole dish.

My rice-pudding dish, Bernadette thought. Jeez, I haven't made rice pudding in a long time.

"Did it have to be a specific ember? Because I couldn't keep that particular one alive all night, so I used the one I got to start a fire at my house," Patrick said, putting the dish on the ground. "This is an ember from that fire." He handed her the oven mitts and the paper bag.

"I think it'll be okay. Patrick, listen, I'm sure your mother will tell you this herself, but she is going to be so incredibly proud of you—that you were able to get this done."

"Actually, it was easier than trying to get my baby brother to eat or get my other brother out of bed."

Bernadette winced, almost reflexively.

"What?" Patrick asked, noticing her scowl.

"Nothing—I mean, well, I'm sure you won't have to do those things anymore," she said, thinking that she and Gerard had been so unfair to Patrick—making him do so many things simply because he was *able* to do them. And then, because she was getting nervous about losing control of her emotions and where this conversation might lead next, she turned to go. "I better run with this."

"Wait—when will my mother be home?"

"Sunday morning, hopefully. It takes three days."

"Three days?" Patrick sighed. "Hey—is your last name Downey?"

Bernadette stopped and turned back to Patrick, stunned by his question. "Why?"

"Well, my social-studies teacher told me there was a girl in one of his other classes named Downey—that was my mother's name before she got married. I thought maybe—"

"Yes, my name is Downey, and you're right, we are related."

"How come we've never met?"

"It's a long story. Maybe your mother can explain it better than I can. . . ." Bernadette shifted her weight, hoping he'd let her go.

"Well, you better hurry. That thing's not going to stay hot forever, either. See you in class?"

"Actually, I had to drop that class." If Bernadette hadn't been holding the hot dish, she would have hugged him. "Thank you so much," she said. "Your mother can't wait to see you." Patrick started to blush again, but turned quickly and walked off, toward school. Then he stopped and turned around.

"What previous life?"

"Excuse me?"

"You said we had met in a previous life. . . ."

"Oh, yes—the one before your mother disappeared," Bernadette called, hurrying away. "Gotta go! This thing's hot!" She did not look back again, but she thought: What a great kid. She had been keeping a list of vows in her head. If I get back to my family, I will not take them for granted. I will be careful about making wishes. I will continue to do sit-ups. Now she added: I will give Patrick a lot more freedom. He's earned it. Then she had another idea.

I bet, she thought, Mom wouldn't mind if I used some of

her coffee-can money to soundproof the garage and buy Patrick a bigger amp. I can tell him it's from her.

She went directly to her mother's house. She had extinguished the fire in the grate before she left so she could start one with the bonfire ember as soon as she got home. As she approached the house now, she looked up at the chimney and realized, though a fire had been burning in the fireplace since the night before her birthday, she had never once noticed a curl of smoke rising from this roof. More magic.

She got the Irish legends book and reread the passage on making soul cakes. It appeared following the footnote on testing for the presence of fairies:

The soul cake cure: If fairies are present and the afflicted party seeks a cure, take the remaining meal and shape it into three oval cakes. Bake the cakes over a hearth that has an ember from a May fire.

The patient must eat each cake on three successive mornings, each with a sprig of watercress. The cakes must be eaten by the fire, taking care that neither cat, dog, nor any other living thing passes between him and the cakes as they are being baked and eaten. After eating the third cake, squeeze the juice of nine gooseberries into a teacup. Throw the tenth berry over the left shoulder. The patient must drink the juice, careful to keep his eyes open while swallowing.

Press nine thorns from the bush at the affected part, throwing the tenth over the left shoulder. On the fourth morning, the patient will be restored. He must not speak to any person about the cure.

Bernadette added water to the meal and pressed the mixture into three small ovals. She laid out the gooseberries, the thorns, and the bag with the watercress in it. She got a cast-iron skillet and a wire rack. Then she went to find her mother.

"Mom, this part about 'press nine thorns at the affected part'?" She showed her mother the book and pointed to the paragraph she meant. "Which part is the affected part?"

"Why, your heart, of course."

"Oh. Of course."

"Are you ready?"

"I'm going to bake the cakes now and eat the first one in the morning."

"I'll have to stay out of your way, then. It's best I not be involved at all. On the last night, be sure to put on bigger clothes. And you'll have to sleep outside—not in the garden, mind you, it's riddled with enchantments. Take some blankets and try to get yourself comfortable on the front porch. And Bernadette, most important . . ."

"Yes?"

"Be sure you are out there before midnight."

"Where will you be?"

"Well, I'll be making myself scarce while you're exorcising the fairies, but after that . . ." Fiona swallowed, as if to compose herself. "After that, I don't know, do I? Try as I might, I can't recall where I was before you called me back here."

"Oh, Mom." Bernadette looked up at her mother. Fiona rarely cried, but Bernadette saw a tear in her eye now. "Are you scared?"

"A wee bit."

"Maybe I shouldn't do this."

"No, you must. It is time for us to say good-bye, though."

Bernadette was dreading this moment, but she, too, knew it was important to say the things she hadn't gotten to say before.

"Mom, until this happened, I didn't realize how much I missed you, how much trouble I had letting go. . . ." Bernadette's words caught in her throat. Her mother moved closer, her thin arms cradling Bernadette.

"Let go, Bernadette. Sell the house. Move on," Fiona said. With her shirtsleeve, she mopped a tear that had rolled down Bernadette's cheek. "There are few truly important choices we get to make in life, but one is choosing to continue it by having children of our own. You've got three powerful reasons to get out of here—four if you count the doctor, and I would. Kiss them for me."

Bernadette burrowed into her mother's body, hugging her tight, so tight she could already feel her slipping away. "I love you, Mom. Will we ever see each other again?"

"Death can't stop a daughter from seeing her mother. Look for me in the love you give your boys," her mother said, pushing her away slightly so she could plant a kiss on Bernadette's forehead, and one on each cheek, and, finally, a small kiss on her lips. "Now go bake your cakes, child."

Bernadette ate a cake for breakfast Thursday, Friday, and Saturday. They could have used some sugar.

Saturday evening, she lifted a teacup from the drain rack by the sink. It took tremendous effort to get liquid from the gooseberries, but she managed a few drops from each. She wished she had her garlic press, because she was concerned she hadn't produced enough juice. She wasn't sure how literally you had to take the laws of magic, but she didn't want to take any chances. She drained the cup with her eyes focused on a dark spot on the ceiling. Hmm, she thought, I wonder if that spot means the roof is leaking somewhere. Standing with her back to the garden at the open kitchen door, she threw one berry over her left shoulder. The wind carried the sound of trick-or-treaters marching up to the next-door neighbor's.

Back inside, she opened her blouse and pressed the thorns against her heart, letting each prick her skin. She stood with her back to the fireplace and threw the tenth thorn over her left shoulder, into the grate.

She went upstairs and took off her corduroy jumpsuit, smoothing the wrinkles from the day's wear. She fastened the snaps over a hanger and hooked it onto the rod in the closet. She wiggled the vent, hopefully for the last time, retrieving her laptop and her overnight bag. She shook out the clothes she had been wearing the night before her birthday—a boxy red sweater and a pair of stretchy black pants. She put them on. The shoulder seams reached down to the middle of her biceps. She rolled up the sleeves, then bent down and turned up the legs of the pants several times.

From the linen closet, she took several blankets. Since she had begun the cakes, her mother had virtually disappeared, though Bernadette had seen her go upstairs to her room Thursday and pad through the kitchen and out the back door Friday, careful not to cross between Bernadette and the hearth where the cakes were keeping warm in the skillet. Saturday, she didn't see her at all, as if she had evaporated, but on the kitchen counter Bernadette found pages and pages of recipes for cures and cordials, soda bread and scones, written in her mother's scratchy handwriting. Bernadette rolled the sheets into a tube and stuck them in the back pocket of her pants. Then she looked around at the house a final time and said good-bye to the emptiness.

Outside, she laid out one blanket on the top step. She had her laptop and her canvas bag, and she covered them and herself with two other blankets. She could not imagine surrendering to sleep under these conditions.

The cul-de-sac was quiet, though a block away, Bernadette could see the stragglers from trick-or-treating heading home. No one had come to her mother's house looking for candy. It probably looked authentically haunted, with its dark rooms and its unmowed grass.

She laid her head down on a blanket and saw something move in the shaggy lawn—a dark rabbit. It looked—well, it looked familiar, like the same rabbit she had seen one day eating something from her mother's garden. It stood there, watching her, its head cocked to the side. She wished she had a carrot to draw the rabbit closer. Later, when Bernadette's eyes could no longer stay open, she felt its soft fur brush her cheek. She fell asleep as the wind was rising to a howl, and in her dreams, she felt the rabbit curl warmly against her.

The sun was breaking over the Cunninghams' house to the east when Bernadette awakened, feeling damp and achy.

She startled to life and quickly pulled back her blanket. She saw long, thick legs encased like sausages in black stretch pants. Little pistons of happiness exploded in her brain and belly. She looked skyward, folded her hands in prayer, and said, "Thank you."

Bernadette pushed herself to stand on wobbly legs. She unrolled her sleeves and her pant legs. She reached her arms up way over her head and stood on tiptoe, stretching. She quietly cried out, "Yippee!" Then she ran down the front steps, threw her arms forward, and did a perfect cartwheel in the long grass.

Patrick

SUNDAY, NOVEMBER 1

The ringing of the telephone awakened Patrick. He lay in the dark, eyes on the ceiling, listening to his father's voice on the phone. He heard him dress, take his keys from the top of his bureau, then head downstairs and out the front door. The car grumbled in the driveway. Somewhere, a woman in pain was waiting for his father to bring her baby into the world.

Patrick got up, sidestepping the candy wrappers around Kevin's bed, litter from the previous night's big haul. He dressed quickly, careful to make no sound. He eased open the bottom drawer of his dresser and took out the red sweater his mother had bought for the Christmas photo the year before.

It was 6 A.M.

In the kitchen, his father had left him a hastily scribbled note:

P—

Gone to the hospital. Hopefully will be back by nine, but please feed Neil.

Love, Dad

Patrick took a twenty-dollar bill from the emergency envelope in the junk drawer. He knew his father wouldn't mind.

Outside the air was bracing and the streets empty. He saw a few smashed pumpkins and toilet paper hanging from a tree. But the neighborhood was sleeping off Halloween, young children up late Saturday night, bedtimes postponed by excitement and sugar rushes.

When he reached the bakery, the sun was just coming up over the Atlantic in the east. Patrick pushed the door open. The warm smell enveloped him. He wouldn't mind working here himself. Maybe his mother could help him get a job— someday. Not yet. It was nice to still be just a customer. The glass cases glistened with chocolate éclairs, napoleons, and raspberry tarts.

"A dozen doughnuts, please," he said to the woman at the counter.

"You want to pick them out?"

"Half custard, half jelly."

The woman slotted the cardboard box together. With a tissue, she nestled the custards on one side and the jellies on the other, lumpy babies in a cardboard crib.

"Anything else?" she asked, securing the flaps in place before winding red-and-white cotton string around the box.

"Yes, a birthday cake. A small one. The strawberry short-cake."

"You want something written on it?"

" 'Happy Birthday, Mom.' No—wait."

She held the cake aloft in the palm of her hand. "You're not sure if it's her birthday?"

"No. Write 'Welcome home, Mom,' instead."

"It's your cake."

It was a small risk, but Patrick had decided to assume that sometime today, the doorbell would ring, he would answer it, and she'd be there. He hadn't told his father or his brothers. He'd have to hide the cake until she arrived. He put the change in his pocket and stacked the smaller box on top of the doughnuts.

Wishing won't make it so, his mother had always told him, but he wasn't just wishing. He was prepared. He had gotten the stuff she needed. He had kept her secret. He had thought of another birthday gift for her, too: his old guitar and a promise to give her lessons.

Patrick was determined there would be a celebration, not only because his mother was home, though that was the biggest reason. But also because, once she was, he could go back to being just twelve again.